Essays in Love

D1334301

'Witty, funny, sophisticated, neatly tied up and full of wise and illuminating insights . . . a very entertaining read' – Gabriele Annan, *Spectator*

'Original, truthful and sometimes funny. It's the kind of book that could become a cult . . . An impressive beginning and a cheerful one' – P. J. Kavanagh

'A wholly unexpected delight' – Glyn Maxwell, *Vogue*

'The pleasure of de Botton's text lies in its meticulous execution; in the wit and stylish irony' – Michael Wright, *The Times*

'*Essays in Love* is an exceedingly smart, sharp first novel . . . De Botton is both trenchantly down-to-earth and sensitively intuitive. And he is funny . . . A talent to watch' – Kathy O'Shaugnessy, *European*

'This is a novel of wit and insight: whatever the state of your love life, it will make entertaining and sometimes painful, sometimes profitable reading' – James Friel, *Time Out*

ALAIN DE BOTTON was born in 1969, educated at Cambridge and lives in London. He is the author of *The Romantic Movement* (1994) and *Kiss & Tell* (1995). His work is translated into fourteen languages.

ALAIN DE BOTTON

Essays in Love

PICADOR

First published 1993 by Macmillan

This edition published 1994 by Picador
an imprint of Macmillan Publishers Ltd
25 Eccleston Place, London SW1W 9NF
and Basingstoke

Associated companies throughout the world

ISBN 0 330 34436 0

9 8

A CIP catalogue record for this book is available from
the British Library.

Typeset by CentraCet Limited, Cambridge
Printed and bound in Great Britain by
Mackays of Chatham plc, Chatham, Kent

TABLE OF CONTENTS

CHAPTER ONE ROMANTIC FATALISM 1

CHAPTER TWO IDEALIZATION 13

CHAPTER THREE THE SUBTEXT OF SEDUCTION 20

CHAPTER FOUR AUTHENTICITY 33

CHAPTER FIVE MIND AND BODY 46

CHAPTER SIX MARXISM 55

CHAPTER SEVEN FALSE NOTES 70

CHAPTER EIGHT LOVE OR LIBERALISM 81

CHAPTER NINE BEAUTY 93

CHAPTER TEN SPEAKING LOVE 102

CHAPTER ELEVEN WHAT DO YOU SEE IN HER? 114

CHAPTER TWELVE SCEPTICISM AND FAITH 122

CHAPTER THIRTEEN INTIMACY 126

CHAPTER FOURTEEN 'I'-CONFIRMATION 137

CHAPTER FIFTEEN INTERMITTENCES OF THE HEART 152

TABLE OF CONTENTS

CHAPTER SIXTEEN THE FEAR OF HAPPINESS 167

CHAPTER SEVENTEEN CONTRACTIONS 177

CHAPTER EIGHTEEN ROMANTIC TERRORISM 188

CHAPTER NINETEEN BEYOND GOOD AND EVIL 198

CHAPTER TWENTY PSYCHO-FATALISM 210

CHAPTER TWENTY-ONE SUICIDE 220

CHAPTER TWENTY-TWO THE JESUS COMPLEX 226

CHAPTER TWENTY-THREE ELLIPSIS 232

CHAPTER TWENTY-FOUR LOVE LESSONS 238

CHAPTER ONE

ROMANTIC FATALISM

1.   The longing for a destiny is nowhere stronger than in our romantic life. All too often forced to share our bed with those who cannot fathom our soul, can we not be forgiven if we believe [contrary to all the rules of our enlightened age] that we are fated one day to meet the man or woman of our dreams? Can we not be excused a certain superstitious faith in a creature who wiii prove the solution to our relentless yearnings? And though our prayers may never be answered, though there may be no end to the dismal cycle of mutual incomprehension, if the heavens should come to take pity on us, then can we really be expected to attribute the encounter with this prince or princess to a mere coincidence? Or can we not for once escape rational censure and read it as nothing other than an inevitable part of our romantic destiny?

2.   One midmorning in early December, with no thought of love or story, I was sitting in the economy section of a British Airways jet making its way from Paris to London. We had recently crossed the Normandy coast, where a blanket of winter cloud had given way to an uninterrupted view of brilliant blue waters. Bored and unable to concentrate, I had picked up the airline magazine, passively imbibing information on resort

hotels and airport facilities. There was something comforting about the flight, the dull background throb of the engines, the hushed grey interior, the candy smiles of the airline employees. A trolley carrying a selection of drinks and snacks was making its way down the aisle and, though I was neither hungry nor thirsty, it filled me with the vague anticipation that meals may elicit in aircraft.

3.   Perhaps rather morbidly, the passenger on my left had taken off her headphones in order to study the safety instruction card placed in the pouch in front of her. It depicted the ideal crash, passengers alighting softly and calmly on land or water, the ladies taking off their high heels, the children dexterously inflating their vests, the fuselage still intact, the kerosene miraculously non-flammable.

4.   'We're all going to die if this thing screws up, so what are these jokers on about?' asked the passenger addressing no one in particular.

'I think perhaps it reassures people,' I replied, for I was her only audience.

'Mind you, it's not a bad way to go, very quick, especially if we hit land and you're sitting in the front. I had an uncle who died in a plane crash once. Has anyone you know ever died like that?'

They hadn't, but I had no time to answer for a stewardess arrived and [unaware of the ethical doubts recently cast on her employers] offered us lunch. I asked for a glass of orange juice and was going to decline a plate of pale sandwiches when my travelling companion whispered to me, 'Take them anyway. I'll eat yours, I'm starving.'

5.   She had chestnut-coloured hair, cut short so that it left the nape of her neck exposed, and large watery green eyes that refused to look into mine. She was wearing a blue blouse and had placed a grey cardigan over her knees. Her shoulders were slim, almost fragile, and the rawness of her nails showed they were often chewed.

'Are you sure I'm not depriving you?'

'Absolutely not.'

'I'm sorry, I haven't introduced myself, my name is Chloe,' she announced and extended her hand across the arm rest with somewhat touching formality.

An exchange of biography followed; Chloe told me she had been in Paris in order to attend a trade fair. For the past year, she had been working as a graphic designer for a fashion magazine in Soho. She had studied at the Royal College of Art, had been born in York, but moved to Wiltshire as a child, and was now [at the age of twenty-three] living alone in a flat in Islington.

6.   'I hope they haven't lost my luggage,' said Chloe as the plane began to drop towards Heathrow. 'Don't you have that fear, that they'll lose your luggage?'

'I don't think about it, but it's happened to me, twice in fact, once in New York, and once in Frankfurt.'

'God, I hate travelling,' sighed Chloe, and bit the end of her index finger. 'I hate arriving even more, I get real arrival angst. After I've been away for a while, I always think something terrible has happened in my absence, a water pipe has burst, or I've lost my job, or my cacti have died.'

'You keep cacti?'

'Several, I went through a phase. Phallic I know, but I spent a winter in Arizona and sort of got fascinated by them. Do you keep pets?'

'I used to have some fish.'

'What happened to them?'

'I was living with a girlfriend a few years ago. I think she got jealous or something, because one day she turned off the thing that ventilates the tank and they all died.'

7. The conversation meandered, affording us glimpses of one another's characters, like the brief vistas one catches on a winding mountain road – this before the wheels hit the tarmac, the engines were thrown into reverse thrust, and the plane taxied towards the terminal, where it disgorged its cargo into the crowded immigration hall. By the time I had collected my luggage and passed through customs, I had fallen in love with Chloe.

8. Until one is actually dead [and then it must be considered impossible], it is difficult to consider anyone as the love of one's life. But only shortly after meeting her, it seemed in no way out of place to think of Chloe in such terms. I cannot with any assurance say why, out of all the available emotions and all their possible recipients, it should suddenly have been love I felt for her. I cannot claim to know the inner dynamics of this process, nor validate these words with anything other than the authority

of lived experience. I can only report that a few days after my return to London, Chloe and I spent the afternoon together. Then, a few weeks before Christmas, we had dinner in a West London restaurant and, as though it was both the strangest and most natural thing to do, ended the evening making love in her apartment. She spent Christmas with her family, I went to Scotland with friends, but we found ourselves calling one another every day, sometimes as many as five times a day, not to say anything in particular, simply because both of us felt that we had never spoken like this to anyone before, that all the rest had been compromise and self-deception, that only now were we finally able to understand and make ourselves understood – that the waiting [messianic in nature] was truly over. I recognized in her the woman I had been clumsily seeking all my life, a being whose qualities had been foreshadowed in my dreams, whose smile and whose eyes, whose sense of humour and whose taste in books, whose anxieties and whose intelligence perfectly matched those of my ideal.

9.   And it was because I came to feel we were so right for one another [she did not just finish my sentences, she completed my life] that I was unable to contemplate the idea that meeting Chloe had simply been a coincidence. I lost the ability to consider the question of predestination with the ruthless scepticism some would say it demanded. Not normally superstitious, Chloe and I seized upon a host of details, however trivial, as confirmation of what intuitively we already felt; *that we had been destined for one another*. We learnt that both of us had been born at around midnight [she at 11.45 p.m., I at 1.15 a.m.] in the same month of an even-numbered year. Both of us had

played clarinet and had had parts in school productions of *A Midsummer Night's Dream* [she had played Helena, I had played an attendant to Theseus]. Both of us had two large freckles on the toe of the left foot and a cavity in the same rear molar. Both of us had a habit of sneezing in bright sunlight and of drawing ketchup out of its bottle with a knife. We even had the same copy of *Anna Karenina* on our shelves [the old Oxford edition] – small details perhaps, but were they not grounds enough on which believers could found a new religion?

10.   Sublimating existence into meaning, we attributed time with a narrative sense it did not inherently possess. Chloe and I mythologized our aircraft encounter into Aphrodite's design, Act I Scene i, of that most classic and mythic narrative configuration – the love story. From the time of each of our births, it seemed as though the giant mind in the sky had been subtly shifting our orbits so that we could have met one day on the Paris–London shuttle. Because it had come true for us, we could overlook the countless stories that fail to occur, romances that never get written because someone misses the plane or loses the phone number. Like historians, we were unmistakably on the side of what had happened, oblivious to the chance nature of every situation, and hence guilty of constructing grand narratives, the Hegels and Spenglers of our own lives. Playing the narrator [the one who comes after the event], we had alchemized the airline meeting into a purposeful event, ascribing to our lives an implausible degree of causality. In so doing, we were guilty of a most mystical, or [to put it more kindly] literary, step.

11. We should of course have been more rational. Neither Chloe nor I flew regularly between the two capitals, nor had been planning our respective trips for any length of time. Chloe had been sent to Paris at the last minute by her magazine after the deputy editor had happened to fall sick, and I had gone only because an architectural assignment in Bordeaux had happened to finish early enough for me to spend a few days there with my sister. The two national airlines running services between Charles de Gaulle and Heathrow offered us a choice of six flights between nine o'clock and lunchtime on our intended day of return. Given that we both wanted to be back in London by the early afternoon of December 6, but were unresolved until the very last minute as to what flight we would end up taking, the mathematical probability at dawn of us both being on the same flight [though not necessarily in adjoining seats] had been a figure of 1 in 36.

12. Chloe later told me that she had intended to take the ten thirty Air France flight, but a bottle of shampoo in her bag had happened to leak as she was checking out of her room, which had meant repacking the bag and wasting a valuable ten minutes. By the time the hotel had produced her bill, cleared her credit card, and found her a taxi, it was already nine fifteen, and the chances that she would make the ten thirty Air France flight had receded. When she reached the airport after heavy traffic near the Porte de la Villette, the flight had finished boarding and, because she did not feel like waiting for the next Air France, she went over to the British Airways terminal, where she booked herself on the ten forty-five plane to London,

on which [for my own set of reasons] I happened also to have a seat.

13. Thereafter, the computer so juggled things that it placed Chloe over the wing of the aircraft in seat 15A and I next to her in seat 15B [see fig 1.1]. What we had ignored when we began speaking over the safety instruction card was the minuscule probability that our discussion would occur at all; as neither of us was likely to fly Club Class, and as there were a hundred and ninety-one economy class seats, and Chloe had been assigned seat 15A, and I, quite by chance, had been assigned seat 15B, the theoretical probability that Chloe and I would be seated next to one another [though the chances of our actually talking to one another could not be calculated], worked itself out as 110 in 17,847, a figure reducible to a probability of 1 in 162.245.

Figure 1.1   British Airways Boeing 767

14. But this was of course only the probability that we would have been seated together if there had been just *one* flight between Paris and London, but as there were six, and as both of us had hesitated between these six, and yet had chosen this one, the probability had to be further multiplied by the original one chance in thirty-six, giving a final probability that Chloe

8

and I would meet one December morning over the English Channel in a British Airways Boeing, as one chance in 5840.82.

[p=1/36–> 110/17,847 = 1/162(.245)–> 1/162.245 × 36 = 1/5840.821]

15. And yet it had happened. The calculation, far from convincing us of the rational arguments, only backed up the mystical interpretation of our fall into love. If the chances behind an event are enormously remote, yet the event occurs nevertheless, may one not be forgiven for invoking a fatalistic explanation? Flipping a coin, a probability of one in two prevents me turning to God to account for a head or a tail. But when it is a question of a probability as small as the one in which Chloe and I were implicated, a probability of 1 in 5840.82, it seemed impossible, from within love at least, that it could have been anything but fate. It would have taken a steady mind to contemplate without superstition the enormous improbability of a meeting that had turned out to alter our lives. Someone [at 30,000 feet] must have been pulling strings in the sky.

16. There are two approaches one can take to account for events lying in the realm of chance. The philosophical view limits itself to primary reasons, adhering to the law of Ockham's razor, stating that reasons behind events must be pared down so they are not multiplied beyond strict causal necessity. This means looking for reasons most immediately explaining what has happened, in my case the probability that Chloe and I had been assigned adjoining seats on the same flight, not the

9

position of Mars in relation to the sun, or the plot structure of a romantic destiny. But the mystical approach cannot resist tampering with wider theories of the universe. A mirror falls off the wall and splinters into a thousand pieces. Why has this happened? What can this mean? For the philosopher, it means nothing more than that a mirror has fallen to the floor, nothing but the fact that a light earthquake and certain forces obeying the laws of physics have conspired [according to a calculable probability] to bring down the mirror at just this point. But for the mystic, the broken mirror is filled with meaning, an ominous sign of no less than seven years' bad luck, divine retribution for a thousand sins and herald of a thousand punishments.

17. In a world where God died a hundred years ago, and computers not oracles predict the future, romantic fatalism veers dangerously towards mysticism. For me to have clung to the idea that Chloe and I had been fated to run into one another on an aeroplane in order then to fall in love, implied attachment to a primitive belief system on the level of tea-leaf reading or crystal-ball gazing. If God did not play dice, He or She certainly did not run a dating service.

18. However, surrounded by chaos, we are understandably led to temper the full horror of contingency by suggesting that certain things happen to us because they have to, thereby giving the mess of life a sustaining purposiveness and direction. Though the dice may roll any number of ways, we frantically draw up patterns of necessity, never more than when it is the inevitability that one day we will fall in love. We are forced to believe that this meeting with our redeemer, objectively haphaz-

ard and hence unlikely, has been pre-written in a scroll slowly unwinding in the sky, and that time must therefore eventually [however reticent it has been till now] reveal to us the figure of our chosen one. What lies behind this tendency to read things as part of a destiny? Perhaps only its opposite, the anxiety of contingency, the fear that the little sense there is in our life is merely created by ourselves, that there is no scroll [and hence no pre-ordained fate awaiting] and that what may or may not be happening to us [who we may or may not be meeting on aeroplanes] has no sense beyond what we choose to attribute to it – in short, the anxiety that there is no God to tell our story, and hence assure our loves.

19.   Romantic fatalism was no doubt a myth and an illusion, but that was no reason to dismiss it as nonsense. Myths may assume an importance that goes beyond their primary message, we don't have to believe in Greek gods in order to know that they tell us something vital about the mind of man. It was absurd to suppose that Chloe and I had been fated to meet, but it was forgivable that we should have thought things were so destined. In our naïve belief, we were only defending ourselves against the idea that we might equally well have begun loving someone else had the airline computer juggled things differently, a thought that was inconceivable when love is so bound up with the uniqueness of the beloved. How could I have imagined that the role Chloe came to play in my life could equally well have been filled by someone else, when it was with her eyes that I had fallen in love, and her way of lighting a cigarette and of kissing, and of answering the phone and combing her hair?

11

20.   Through romantic fatalism, we avoid the unthinkable thought that the need to love is always prior to our love for anyone in particular. Our choice of partner necessarily operates within the bounds of who we happen to meet and given different bounds, different flights, different historical periods or events, it might not have been Chloe I would have loved at all – something I could not contemplate now that it was her I had actually begun to love. My mistake had been to confuse a destiny to love with a destiny to love a given person. It was the error of thinking that Chloe, rather than love, was inevitable.

21.   But my fatalistic interpretation of the beginning of our story was at least proof of one thing; that I was in love with Chloe. The moment when I would feel our meeting or not meeting was in the end only an accident, only a probability of 1 in 5840.82, would also be the moment when I would have ceased to feel the absolute necessity of a life with her – and thereby have ceased to love her.

CHAPTER TWO

IDEALIZATION

1.   'Seeing through people is so easy, and it gets you nowhere,' remarked Elias Canetti, hinting at how effortlessly and yet how uselessly we may find fault with others. May we not therefore fall in love partly out of a momentary will to suspend seeing through people, even at the cost of blinding ourselves a little in the process? If cynicism and love lie at opposite ends of a spectrum, do we not sometimes fall in love in order to escape the debilitating cynicism to which we are prone? Is there not in every *coup de foudre* a certain wilful exaggeration of the qualities of the beloved, an exaggeration that distracts us from disillusion by focusing our energies on a given face, in which we are briefly and miraculously able to believe?

2.   I lost Chloe amidst the throng at passport control, but found her again in the luggage reclaim area. She was struggling to push a trolley cursed with a stubborn inclination to steer to the right, though the Paris carousel was to the far left of the hall. Because my trolley had no mind of its own, I walked over and offered it to her, but she refused, saying one should remain loyal to trolleys, however stubborn, and that strenuous physical exercise was no bad thing after a flight. Indirectly [via the

13

Karachi arrival], we made it to the Paris carousel, already crowded with faces grown involuntarily familiar since boarding at Charles de Gaulle. The first pieces of luggage had begun to tumble down on to the jointed rubber matting, and faces peered anxiously at the moving display to locate their possessions.

3.   'Have you ever been arrested at customs?' asked Chloe.
'Not yet. Have you?'
'Not really, I once made a confession. This Nazi asked me if I had anything to declare, and I said yes, even though I wasn't carrying anything illegal.'
'So why did you say you were?'
'I don't know, I felt sort of guilty: I have this awful tendency to confess to things I haven't done. I've always had fantasies about giving myself up to the police for some crime I didn't commit.'

4.   'By the way, don't judge me on my luggage,' said Chloe as we continued to watch and wait while others got lucky, 'I bought it at the last minute in this horrible shop on the rue de Rennes. It's a horrendous thing.'
'Wait till you see mine. Except that I don't even have an excuse. I've been carrying mine around for over five years.'
'Can I ask you a favour? Could you look after my trolley while I look for the loo? I'll just be a minute. Oh, and if you see a pink carrier bag with a luminous green handle, that'll be mine.'

5.   A little later, I watched Chloe walk back towards me across the hall, wearing what I later learnt was her usual pained

and slightly anxious expression. She had a face that looked permanently near tears, her eyes carried the fear of someone about to be told a piece of very bad news. Something about her made one want to comfort her, offer her reassurance [or a simple hand to hold].

'Has it come yet?' she asked.

'No, nor has mine, but there are still a lot of people around. For at least another five minutes, there's probably no excuse for paranoia.'

'What a blow,' smiled Chloe and looked down at her feet.

6.   Love was something I sensed very suddenly, shortly after she had embarked on what promised to be a very long and very boring story [indirectly sparked by the arrival of the Athens flight in the carousel next to us] about a holiday that she had taken one summer with her brother in Rhodes. While Chloe talked, I watched her hands fiddling with the belt of her beige woollen coat [a pair of freckles were collected below the index finger] and realized [as if it had been the most self-evident of truths] that I loved her. I could not avoid the conclusion that, however awkward it was that she rarely finished her sentences, or was somewhat anxious and had not perhaps the best taste in earrings, *she was adorable*. It was a moment of complete idealization, dependent as much on an inexcusable emotional immaturity as on the elegance of her coat, my jet-lag, what I had eaten for breakfast and the depressing interior of the Terminal Four baggage area, against which her beauty showed up so starkly.

7.   *The island was packed with tourists, but we rented motorcycles and* . . . Chloe's holiday story was dull, but its dullness was no

longer a criterion of judgement. I had ceased to consider it according to the secular logic of ordinary conversations. I was no longer concerned to locate within its syntax either intellectual insight or poetic truth, what mattered was not so much *what* she was saying, as the fact *she* was saying it – and that I had decided to find perfection in everything she might choose to utter. I felt ready to follow her into every anecdote [*There was this shop that served fresh olives . . .*], I was ready to love every one of her jokes that had missed its punch-line, every reflection that had lost its thread. I felt ready to abandon self-absorption for the sake of total empathy, to follow Chloe into each of her possible selves, to catalogue every one of her memories, to become a historian of her childhood, to learn of all her loves, fears and hatreds – everything that could possibly have played itself out within her mind and body had suddenly grown fascinating.

8.   Then the luggage arrived, hers only a few cases behind mine, we loaded it on to the trolleys and walked out through the green channel.

9.   What is so frightening is the extent to which one may idealize another, when one has such trouble even tolerating oneself – *because* one has such trouble . . . I must have realized Chloe was only human [with all the implications carried by the word] but could I not be forgiven – with all the stress of travel and existence – for my desire to suspend such a thought? Every fall into love involves [to adapt Oscar Wilde] the triumph of hope over self-knowledge. We fall in love hoping that we will not find in the other what we know is in ourselves – all the

cowardice, weakness, laziness, dishonesty, compromise and brute stupidity. We throw a cordon of love around the chosen one, and decide that everything that lies within it will somehow be free of our faults and hence lovable. We locate inside another a perfection that eludes us within ourselves, and through union with the beloved, hope somehow to maintain [against evidence of all self-knowledge] a precarious faith in the species.

10.   Why did awareness of this not prevent my fall into love? Because the illogicality and childishness of my desire did not outweigh my need to believe. I knew the void that romantic illusion could fill, I knew the exhilaration that came from identifying someone, anyone, as admirable. Long before I had even laid eyes on Chloe, I must have needed to find in the face of another a perfection I had never caught sight of within myself.

11.   'May I check your bags, sir?' asked the customs man. 'Do you have anything to declare, any alcohol, cigarettes, firearms . . .?'

Like genius and Wilde, I wanted to say, *'Only my love,'* but my love was not a crime, not yet at least.

'Shall I wait with you?' asked Chloe.

'Are you together with madam?' enquired the customs officer.

Afraid of presumption, I answered no, but asked Chloe if she'd wait for me on the other side.

12.   Love reinvents our needs with unique speed and specificity. My impatience with the customs ritual indicated that Chloe,

who I had not known existed a few hours ago, had already acquired the status of a craving. This was not hunger, where the signs are gradual, where there is a recognizable chronology to the need, arriving cyclically at meal times. I felt I would die if I missed her on the other side of the hall – die for the sake of someone who had only entered my life at eleven thirty that morning.

13.   If the fall into love happens so rapidly, it is perhaps because the wish to love has preceded the beloved – the need has invented its solution. The appearance of the beloved is only the second stage of a prior [but largely unconscious] need to love *someone* – our hunger for love moulding their features, our desire crystallizing around them. [But the honest side of us will never let the deception go unchallenged. There will always be moments when we will doubt whether our lover exists in reality as we imagine them in our minds – or whether they are not just a hallucination we have invented to prevent the inevitable loveless collapse.]

14.   Chloe had waited, but we only spent a moment together before parting again. She had left her car in the car park, I had to take a taxi to pick up some papers from my office – it was one of those awkward moments when both parties hesitate whether or not to continue with the story.

'I'll give you a call some time,' I said casually, 'we could go and buy some luggage together.'

'That's a good idea,' said Chloe, 'have you got my number?'

'I'm afraid I already memorized it, it was written on your baggage tag.'

'You'd make a good detective, I hope your memory is up to it. Well, it was nice meeting you,' said Chloe extending a hand.

'Good luck with the cacti,' I called after her as I watched her head for the lifts, the trolley still veering madly to the right.

15.   In the taxi on the way into town, I felt a curious sense of loss, of sadness. Could this really be love? To speak of love after we had barely spent a morning together was to encounter charges of romantic delusion and semantic inaccuracy. Yet we can only ever fall in love without knowing who we have fallen in love with. *The initial movement is necessarily founded on ignorance.* So if I called it love in the face of so many doubts, both psychological and epistemological, it was perhaps out of a belief that the word could never be used *accurately*. As love was not a place, or colour, or chemical, but all three of these and more, or none of these and less, might not everyone speak and decide as they wished when it came to this province? Did this question not lie beyond the academic realm of true and false? Love or simple obsession? Who, if not time [which was its own liar] could possibly begin to tell?

CHAPTER THREE

THE SUBTEXT
OF SEDUCTION

1.   For those in love with certainty, seduction is no territory in which to stray. Every smile and every word reveals itself as an avenue leading to a dozen if not twelve thousand possibilities. Gestures and remarks that in normal life [that is, *life without love*] can be taken at face value now exhaust dictionaries with possible definitions. And, for the seducer at least, the doubts reduce themselves to one central question, faced with the trepidation of a criminal awaiting sentence: *Does s/he, or does s/he not, desire me?*

2.   Unable to possess, the thought of Chloe did not stop haunting me in the days that followed. I could not account for this desire, the only explanation comprehensive enough would have been to mutely point to the desired person herself [thereby echoing Montaigne's reasons for his friendship with La Boétie; because she was she, and I was I]. Though under pressure to complete plans for an office near King's Cross, my mind drifted irresponsibly but irresistibly back to her. There was a need to circle around this object of adoration, she kept breaking into consciousness with the urgency of a matter that had to be addressed, though these thoughts were part of no agenda, they were [objectively speaking] desperately uninteresting, having no

development or point to them, they were pure desire. Some of these Chloe-thoughts ran like this, '*Ah, how wonderful she is, how nice it would be to . . .*'

Others were static images:

[i] Chloe framed by the aircraft window
[ii] Her watery green eyes
[iii] Her teeth biting briefly into her lower lip
[iv] Her accent while saying: '*That's strange.*'
[v] The tilt of her neck when yawning
[vi] The gap between her two front teeth
[vii] Her handshake

3.   If only consciousness had summoned such diligence for her phone number, for the unfortunate set of digits had altogether evaporated from memory [a memory that felt its time better spent replaying images of Chloe's lower lip]. Was it (*071*)

607 9187
    609 7187
        601 7987
            690 7187
                610 7987
                    670 9817
                        687 7187?

4.   The first call did not answer my desire, miscommunication the peril of all seduction. *609 7187* was not the beloved's abode but the number of a funeral parlour off Upper Street – though the establishment did not reveal itself as such till the end of a

confused conversation, in the course of which I learnt that *After Life* also had an employee called Chloe, who was summoned to the phone and spent agonizing minutes trying to place my name [eventually identifying me as a customer who had made enquiries into urns] before the confusion of names was cleared up on both sides and I hung up, red-faced, drenched with sweat, nearer to death than life.

5.   When I finally reached my Chloe at work the following day, she too seemed to have relegated me to the after-life [yet what was there to relegate, outside my overripe imagination?].

'Things are crazy around here now. Can you hold for a minute?' she asked secretarially.

I held, offended. Whatever intimacy I had imagined, back in office space, we were strangers, my desire brutally out of place, an unwelcome intrusion into Chloe's working day.

'Listen, I'm sorry,' she said, coming back on the line, 'I really can't talk now. We're preparing a supplement that's going to press tomorrow. Can I call you back? I'll try and reach you either at home or in the office when things calm down, OK?'

6.   The telephone becomes an instrument of torture in the demonic hands of the beloved who does not call. The story lies in the hands of the dialler, the receiver loses narrative control, can only follow, answer when called. The telephone coiled me into the passive role; in the traditional sexuality of the telephone exchange, the feminine receiver to Chloe's masculine call. It forced me to be ready to answer at all times, it lent an oppressive teleology to my movements. The machine's moulded plastic

surfaces, its user-friendly redial buttons, its coloured design, none of this indicated the cruelty that its mystery concealed, the lack of clue it gave as to when it [and hence I] would be brought to life.

7.   I would have preferred a letter. When she called a week later, I had rehearsed my speech too often to deliver it. I was caught unprepared, pacing the bathroom naked while cleaning my ears with a cotton bud and keeping an eye on the flow of the bath. I ran over to the phone in the bedroom. The voice can only ever be a sketch unless it is learnt, and hence acted. Mine carried with it a tension, an excitement and an anger that I might more skilfully have erased from the page. But the telephone was no word-processor, it gives the speaker only a single chance.

'It's nice to hear from you,' I said idiotically. 'Let's have lunch or dinner, or whatever you like,' the voice cracking a little over the second *or*. How invulnerable the word would have been next to speech, the author could have been made impregnable, hard, grammatically powerful [those who cannot have their say turn to the pen]. Instead of the *author*, there was only this stumbling, leaking, needy, cracking *speaker*.

8.   'I really can't do lunch this week.'
'Well, how about dinner?'
'Dinner? Let me see, ehm, well [pause], I'm just looking at my diary here, and you know, that's looking difficult too.'
'You make the Prime Minister's schedule look light.'
'I'm sorry. Things are really bad around here. I tell you

what though, can you take the afternoon off? This afternoon, we could meet at my office and take a trip around the National Gallery, or whatever you like, go to the park or something.'

9.   Questions pursued me throughout seduction, questions relating to the unmentionable subtext of every word and action. What did Chloe think as we made our way to Trafalgar Square from her office in Bedford Street? The evidence was tantalizingly ambiguous. On the one hand, Chloe had been happy to take the afternoon to tour a museum with a man she had only briefly met in an aeroplane the week before. But on the other, there was nothing in her behaviour to suggest this was anything but an opportunity for an intelligent discussion on art and architecture. Perhaps all this was simply friendship, a maternal, sexless bond of a female for a male. Suspended between innocence and collusion, Chloe's every gesture had become imbued with maddening significance. Did she know that I desired her? Did she desire me? Was I correct in detecting traces of flirtation at the ends of her sentences and the corners of her smiles, or was this merely my own desire projected into the face of innocence?

10.   The museum was crowded at this time of year, so it was a while before we were able to deposit our coats in the cloakroom and make our way up the stairs. We began with the early Italians, though my thoughts [I had lost all perspective, they had yet to find theirs] were not with them. Before *The Virgin and Child with Saints*, Chloe turned to remark that she had always had a thing about Signorelli, and, because it seemed appropriate, I invented a passion for Antonello's *Christ Crucified*. She

24

looked thoughtful, immersed in the canvases, oblivious to the noise and activity in the gallery. I followed a few paces behind her, trying to focus on the paintings, but unable to pierce the third dimension, able to see them only in the context of Chloe looking at them, art through life.

11.   At one point, in the second and more crowded Italian room [1500–1600] we stood so close together that my hand came to touch hers. She did not draw away, and nor did I, so that for a moment [our eyes glued to the canvas opposite], I stood with the feel of Chloe's skin suffusing my body, melting with a sense of illicit pleasure, a voyeuristic thrill because derived without permission, the other's gaze directed elsewhere – though perhaps not wholly unaware. The canvas opposite was by Bronzino, *An Allegory of Venus and Cupid*, Cupid kissing his mother Venus while she surreptitiously removes one of his arrows, beauty blinding love, symbolically disarming the boy of his potency.

12.   Then Chloe moved her hand, turned and said, 'I love those little figures in the background, the little nymphs and angry gods and stuff. Do you understand all the symbolism?'

'Not really, beside it being Venus and Cupid.'

'I didn't even know that, so you're one up on me. I wish I'd read more about ancient mythology,' she continued, 'I keep telling myself I'm going to read more about it, then I never get round to it. But actually, I sort of like looking at things and not knowing quite what they mean.'

She turned to face the painting again, her hand once more brushing against mine.

13.   Her action could have meant more or less anything, it was an empty space onto which one could decide to attach almost any intention from desire to innocence. Was this a piece of subtle symbolism [subtler than Bronzino's and less documented] that would one day allow me [like Cupid on the wall] to reach over and kiss her, or an innocent, unconscious spasm by a tired arm muscle?

14.   As soon as one begins looking for signs of mutual attraction, then everything that the beloved says or does can be taken to mean almost anything. And the more I looked for signs, the more there were of them to read. In every movement of Chloe's body, there seemed to be potential evidence of desire – in the way she straightened her skirt [as we crossed into Early Northern Painting], or coughed by van Eyck's *The Marriage of Giovanni Arnolfini*, or handed me the catalogue in order to rest her head on her hand. And when I listened closely to her conversation, it too revealed itself as a minefield of clues – was I wrong to read a degree of flirtation in her remark that she was tired or her suggestion we look for a bench?

15.   We sat down and Chloe stretched her legs, black stockings that tapered elegantly down to a pair of loafers. It was impossible to place her gestures into a correct lexical framework – had a woman allowed her leg to similarly brush against mine in the Underground, I would not have given it a second thought – it was the difficulty of trying to understand a gesture whose meaning was not imminent in itself, but could only be ascribed to it by its context, by its reader [and what a biased reader I was]. Opposite us hung Cranach's *Cupid Complaining to Venus*.

26

This Northern Venus looked enigmatically down at us, oblivious to poor Cupid, being stung by bees whose honey he had tried to steal, the messenger of love getting his fingers burnt. Symbols.

16.   It was desire that had turned me into this detective, a relentless hunter for clues that would have been ignored had I been less afflicted. It was desire that made me into a romantic paranoiac, *reading meaning into everything*. Desire had transformed me into a decoder of symbols, an interpreter of the landscape [and therefore a potential victim of the pathetic fallacy]. Yet whatever my impatience, nor were these questions free of the inflaming power of all things enigmatic. The ambiguity promised either salvation or damnation, but demanded a lifetime to reveal itself. And the longer I hoped, the more the person I hoped for became exalted, miraculous, perfect, worth hoping for. The very delay helped to increase desirability, an excitement that instant gratification could never have provided. Had Chloe simply shown her cards, the game would have lost its charm. However much I resented it, I recognized that things needed to remain unsaid. The most attractive are not those who allow us to kiss them at once [we soon feel ungrateful] or those who never allow us to kiss them [we soon forget them], but those who coyly lead us between the two extremes.

17.   Venus felt like a drink, so she and Cupid headed for the stairs. In the cafeteria, Chloe took one of the trays and pushed it along the steel railing.

'Do you want tea?' she asked.

'Yeah, but I'll get it.'

'Don't be silly, I'll get it.'

'Please let me do it.'

'Look, thanks, but 80p won't break me.'

We sat at a table with a view of Trafalgar Square below, the lights of the Christmas tree lending an incongruously festive atmosphere to the urban scene. We began talking of art, and from there we moved on to artists, and from artists we moved to get a second cup of tea and a cake, then moved on to beauty, and from beauty we went to love, and at love we stopped.

'I don't understand,' asked Chloe, 'you do or you don't think that there's such a thing as real, lasting love?'

'What I'm trying to say is that it's a very subjective thing, that it's silly to suppose that there is an objectively verifiable thing as "real love", it's tricky to distinguish between passion and love, infatuation and love or whatever, because it all depends on where you're standing.'

'You're right. [pause] Don't you find this cake disgusting though? We should never have bought it.'

'It was your idea.'

'I know. But [Chloe ran her hand through her hair] you know seriously, coming back to what you asked me earlier, whether the romantic is anachronistic or not? I mean, if you asked most people straight off if they thought so, they'd no doubt say it was. But that's not necessarily true. It's just the way they defend themselves against what they truly want. They sort of believe in it, and then pretend they don't until they have to or are allowed to. I think most people would throw away all their cynicism if they could, the majority just never get the chance.'

28

18.   Nothing of what she said could I take at face value, I clung instead to the underbelly of her words, sure the meaning lay there rather than in its obvious location, interpreting instead of listening. We were talking of love, my Venus idly stirring her now cold tea, but what did this conversation mean for *us*? Who were these 'most people' she spoke of? Was *I* the man who would dispel her cynicism? What did this talk of love say of the relationship between the two speakers? Again, no clues. The language was cautiously unself-referential. We talked abstractly of love, ignoring that lying on the table was not the nature of love *per se*, but the burning question of who we were [and would be] to one another.

19.   Or was this a ridiculous suggestion? Was there nothing on the table but a half-eaten carrot cake and two cups of tea? Was Chloe perhaps being as abstract as she wished, meaning precisely what she was saying, the diametrical opposite of the first rule of flirtation, *where what is said is never what is meant*? How hard it was to keep a level head, when Cupid was such a biased interpreter, when it was so clear what he wanted to be true? Was he attributing to Chloe an emotion that only he felt? Was he guilty of the age old error whereby the thought that *I desire you* is mistakenly equated with the corresponding thought that *You desire me*?

20.   We helped to define our positions by reference to others. Chloe had a friend at work who was always falling in love with unsuitable types, a courier was playing the current victimizer.

'I mean, why does she give a minute of her time to someone about three thousand times more stupid than her, who doesn't even have the decency to treat her well, and who basically, and I've told her this, is just using her for sex? And that's fine if she wanted to use him for sex as well, but it's clear she doesn't, so she's just sort of getting the worst of both worlds.'

'It sounds terrible.'

'Yeah, well, it's just really sad. One has to go into relationships with both parties being equal, ready to give as much as one another – not with one person wanting a quick fling and the other wanting real love. And I think that's where all the agony comes from, that there's an imbalance, where people are just not sure enough of themselves or what they want out of life or whatever.'

21.   Tentatively, we plotted our orientations and definitions. We did so in the most tortuous ways, we asked each other 'What does *one* look for in love?' – this 'one' embodying a subtle linguistic abdication of involvement. But though such rituals could have been labelled games, they were both very serious and very useful. These doubts, this lack of resolution [Yes/No?] had a certain logic. Even if Chloe might one day mean 'yes', the ritual of proceeding from A to B via Z had advantages over direct communication. It minimized offending an unwilling partner, and eased a willing one more slowly into the prospect of mutual desire. The threat of the great 'I like you' could be softened by adding, 'but not so much that I will let you know it directly . . .'

22.   We were involved in a game that allowed us to deny as long as possible all involvement in its process, a game whose

principal rule stated that it should be played as though it were not being played, both parties proceeding as though unaware of its existence. We spoke a language that used ordinary words but gave them new meanings, exploiting the tension between coded and ordinary signification:

> Code *'People should be less cynical about love'*
> = Message *'Give up your cynicism for me.'*

It was akin to a wartime code that allowed us to talk as long as possible without the risk of one or the other's desire being left humiliatingly unreciprocated. If the Nazi commanders had burst in on the room, the Allied agents could easily have claimed they had merely been radioing passages of Shakespeare, not transmitting documents of the greatest sensitivity [*I desire you*] – for there was nothing in what Chloe and I were actually *saying* that could directly implicate us. If the signs of seduction are so slight as to be deniable [a mere brush of the hand or look that lingers a fraction too long], then who is to say it is even seduction we are talking about?

23. There could be no better way than this to ease the tremendous risks involved whenever two mouths undertake the long and perilous journey towards each other, risks that reduce themselves to a central danger, *that one will confess one's desire and see it rejected*.

24. Because it was past five thirty and her office would now have closed down, I asked Chloe whether she might not after all be free to have dinner with me that night. She smiled at the suggestion, looked briefly out of the window at a bus heading

past St Martin-in-the-Fields, then looked back and, staring at the ashtray, said, '*No, thanks, that would really be impossible.*' Then, just as I was ready to despair, she blushed.

25.   It is because shyness is the perfect answer to the fundamental doubts within seduction that it is so often invoked to explain the paucity of clear evidence of desire. Faced with the ambiguous signals one receives from the beloved, what better explanation than to put this lack of commitment down to shyness – *the beloved desires, but is too shy to say so*. Its invocation betrays all the hallmarks of a hallucinating mind, for is there not always evidence for shyness in someone's behaviour? It only takes a blush, silence or nervous laugh to legitimate its presence, and therefore the seducer who wishes to call his victim shy will never be disappointed. It is a foolproof method for turning the absence of a sign into a presence, a way of turning a negative into a positive. It even suggests that the shy person is more desirous than the confident one, that the strength of the shy person's desire can be attested by the difficulty of expression.

26.   'My God, I've just forgotten something terrible,' said Chloe, offering an alternative explanation for the blush, 'I was supposed to call the printer this afternoon. Shit. I can't believe I forgot to do that. I'm losing my head.'

The lover offered his sympathy.

'But look, about dinner, we'll have to do it another time. I'd love that, I really would. It's just difficult at the moment, but I'll give my diary another look and call you tomorrow, I promise, and maybe we can fix it up for some time before the weekend.'

CHAPTER FOUR

AUTHENTICITY

1. It is one of the ironies of love that it is easiest to confidently seduce those we are least attracted to, the seriousness of desire stalling the necessary games of insouciance, attraction eliciting a sense of inferiority compared with the perfection we have located in the beloved. My love for Chloe meant I had lost all belief in my own worthiness. Who could *I* be next to *her*? Was it not the greatest honour for her to have agreed to this dinner, to have dressed so elegantly ['*Is this all right?*' she'd asked in the car, '*it had better be, because I'm not changing a sixth time*'], let alone that she be willing to respond to some of the things that might fall [if ever I recovered my tongue] from my unworthy lips?

2. It was Friday night and Chloe and I were seated at a corner table of *Les Liaisons Dangereuses*, a French restaurant that had recently opened at the end of the Fulham Road. There could have been no more appropriate setting for Chloe's beauty, the chandeliers throwing soft shadows across her face, the light green walls matching her light green eyes. And yet, as though struck dumb by the angel that faced me across the table, I found [only minutes after an animated conversation] that I had lost all capacity either to think or speak, able only to

silently draw invisible patterns on the starched white tablecloth and take unnecessary sips of bubbled water from a large glass goblet.

3.   Out of this perceived inferiority emerged the need to take on a personality that was not directly my own, a seducing self that would locate and respond to the demands of this superior being. Did love condemn me not to be myself? Perhaps not for ever, but, if it was to be taken seriously, it did at this stage of seduction, for the seducing position was one which led me to ask: *What would appeal to her?* rather than: *What appeals to me?* I asked: *How would she perceive my tie?* rather than *How do I judge it?* Love forced me to look at myself as through the imagined eyes of the beloved. Not: *Who am I?*, but: *Who am I for her?* And in the reflexive movement of that question, my self could not help but grow tinged with a certain bad faith and inauthenticity.

4.   This inauthenticity did not necessarily manifest itself in flagrant lies or exaggerations. It simply involved trying to anticipate everything Chloe might want, so that I could take on the accent the part demanded.

'Would you like some wine?' I asked her.

'I don't know, would you like wine?' she asked back.

'I really don't mind, if you feel like it,' I replied.

'It's as you please, whatever you want,' she continued.

'Either way is fine with me.'

'I agree.'

'So should we have it or not?'

'Well, I don't think *I'll* have any,' ventured Chloe.

'You're right, I don't feel like any either,' I concurred.
'Let's not have wine then,' she concluded.
'Great, so we'll just stick with the water.'

5.   Though authentic selfhood has as its prerequisite the ability to achieve a stable identity irrespective of company, the evening had developed into an inauthentic attempt to locate and shape myself according to Chloe's desires. What did she expect from a man? What were the tastes and orientations according to which I should adjust my behaviour? If staying true to oneself is deemed an essential criterion of moral self-hood, then seduction had led me to resolutely fail the ethical test. Why had I lied about my feelings towards a delicious looking selection of wines, prominently advertised on a black-board above Chloe's head? Because my choice had suddenly seemed inadequate and crude next to her mineral thirst. Seduction had split me into two, into a true [alcoholic] self, and a false [aquatic] one.

6.   The first course arrived, arranged on plates with the symmetry of a formal French garden.

        'It looks too beautiful to touch,' said Chloe [how I knew the feeling], 'I've never eaten grilled tuna like this before.'

        We began to eat, but the only sound was that of cutlery against china. There seemed to be nothing to say: Chloe had been my only thought for too long, but the one thought that at this moment I could not share. Silence was a damning indict-ment. A silence with an unattractive person implies they are the boring one. A silence with an attractive one leaves you certain it is *you* who are impossibly dull.

7.   Silence and clumsiness could perhaps be forgiven as rather pitiful proof of desire. It being easy enough to seduce someone towards whom one feels indifferent, the clumsiest seducers could generously be deemed the most genuine. Not to find the right words may ironically be proof that the right words are meant [if only they could be said]. When in that other *Liaisons*, the Marquise de Merteuil writes to the Vicomte de Valmont, she faults him on the fact that his love letters are too perfect, too logical to be the words of a true lover, whose thoughts will be disjointed and for whom the fine phrase will always elude. Language trips up on love, desire lacks articulacy [but how willingly I would at that moment have swapped my constipation for the Vicomte's vocabulary].

8.   Given my wish to seduce Chloe, it was essential that I find out more about her. How could I abandon my true self unless I knew what false self to adopt? But this was no easy task, a reminder that understanding another requires hours of careful attention and interpretation, teasing a coherent character from a thousand words and actions. Unfortunately, the patience and intelligence required went far beyond the capacities of my anxious, infatuated mind. I behaved like a reductive social psychologist, eager to press a person into simple definitions, unwilling to apply the care of a novelist to capturing the polyvalence of human nature. Over the first course, I blundered with heavy-handed, interview-like questions; What do you like to read? [*'Joyce, Henry James*, Cosmo *if there's time'*], Do you like your job? [*'All jobs are pretty crappy, don't you think?'*], What country would you live in if you could live anywhere? [*'I'm fine here, anywhere where I don't have to change the plug for my*

36

hairdryer'], What do you like to do on weekends? ['*Go to the movies on Saturday, on Sunday, stock up on chocolate for getting depressed with in the evening.*']

9.   Behind such clumsy questions [with every one I asked, I seemed to get further from knowing her], there was an impatient attempt to get to the most direct question of all, '*Who are you?*' [and hence '*Who should I be?*'] But such a direct approach was naturally doomed to failure, and the more bluntly I pursued it, the more my subject escaped through the net, letting me know what newspaper she read and music she liked, but not thereby enlightening me as to 'who' she was – a reminder, if ever one needed it, of the 'I''s capacity to elude itself.

10.   Chloe hated talking about herself. Perhaps her most obvious feature was a certain modesty and self-deprecation. Whenever the conversation led her to talk on the subject, Chloe did so in the harshest terms. It would not simply be 'I' or 'Chloe', but '*a basket-case like me*' or '*the winner of the Ophelia award for quiet nerves.*' Her self-deprecation was all the more attractive for it seemed free of the veiled appeals of self-pitying people, the double-take self-deprecation of the *I'm so stupid/No, you're not* variety.

11.   Her childhood had not been pleasant, but she was stoic about the matter ['*I hate childhood dramatizations that make Job look like he got off lightly*']. She had been born into a financially comfortable home. Her father ['*All his problems started when his parents called him Barry*'] had been an academic, a professor of

law, her mother ['*Claire*'] had for a time run a flower shop. Chloe was the middle child, a girl sandwiched between two favoured and faultless boys. When her older brother died of leukaemia shortly after her eighth birthday, her parents' grief expressed itself as anger at their daughter who, slow at school and sulky around the house, had obstinately clung to life instead of their darling son. She grew up guilty, filled with a sense of blame for what had happened, feelings that her mother did little to alleviate. She liked to pick on a person's weakest characteristics and not let go – so Chloe was forever reminded of how badly she performed at school compared to the dead brother, of how gauche she was, and of how disreputable her friends were [criticisms that were not particularly true, but that grew more so with every mention]. Chloe had turned to her father for affection, but the man was as closed with his emotions as he was open with his legal knowledge, which he would pedantically share with her as a substitute, until adolescence when Chloe's frustration with him turned to anger and she openly defied him and everything he stood for [it was fortunate that I had not chosen the legal profession].

12.   Of past boyfriends, only hints emerged over the meal: one had worked as motorcycle mechanic in Italy and had treated her very badly, another, who she had mothered, had ended up in jail for possession of drugs, one had been an analytical philosopher at London University ['*You don't have to be Freud to see he was the daddy I never went to bed with*'], another a test-car driver for Rover ['*To this day I can't explain that one. I think I liked his Birmingham accent*']. But no clear picture was emerging and therefore the picture of her ideal man forming in my head

38

needed constant readjustment. There were things she praised and condemned within sentences of each other, forcing me into a frantic rewriting of the self I wanted to suggest. At one moment she seemed to be praising emotional vulnerability, and at the next, damning it in favour of independence. Whereas honesty was at one point extolled as the supreme value, adultery was at another justified on account of the greater hypocrisy of marriage.

13.   The complexity of her views led to a certain schizophrenia in mine. What sides of myself should I release? How could I avoid alienating her without appearing impossibly bland? While we ate our way through the courses [obstacle courses for young Valmont], I found myself tentatively putting forward one opinion only to subtly alter it a minute later to align it with hers. Every one of Chloe's questions was terrifying, for it might unwittingly contain something that would irrevocably offend her. The main course [the duck for me, the salmon for her] was a marshland sowed with mines – did I think two people should live solely for one another? Had my childhood been difficult? Had I ever been truly in love? What had it been like? Was I an emotional or a cerebral person? Who had I voted for in the last election? What was my favourite colour? Did I think women were more unstable than men?

14.   Because it involves the risk of alienating those who do not agree with what one is saying, originality proved wholly beyond me. I merely adjusted myself to whatever I judged Chloe might feel. If she liked tough men, I would be tough, if she liked windsurfing, I would be a windsurfer, if she hated chess, I

would hate chess. My idea of what she wanted from a lover could have been compared to a tight-fitting suit and my true self to a fat man, so that the evening was a process resembling a fat man trying to fit into a suit that is too small for him. There was a desperate attempt to repress the bulges that did not fit the cut of the fabric, to shrink my waist and hold my breath so the material would not tear. It was not surprising if my posture was not as spontaneous as I might have liked. How can a fat man in a suit too small for him feel spontaneous? He is so frightened the suit will split, he is forced to sit in complete stillness, holding his breath and praying he can get through the evening without disaster. Love had crippled me.

15. Chloe was facing a different dilemma, for it was time for dessert, and though she had only one choice, she had more than one desire.

'What do you think, the chocolate or the caramel?' she asked [traces of guilt appearing on her forehead]. 'Maybe you can get one and I'll get the other and then we can share.'

I felt like neither, I was not digesting properly, but that was not the point.

'I just love chocolate, don't you?' asked Chloe. 'I can't understand people who don't like chocolate. I was once going out with a guy, this guy Robert I was telling you about, and I was never really comfortable with him, but I couldn't work out why. Then one day it all became clear: he didn't like chocolate. I mean he didn't just not love it, this guy actually hated it. You could have put a bar in front of him and he wouldn't have touched it. That kind of thinking is so far removed from anything I can relate to, you know. Well after that, you can imagine, it was clear we had to break up.'

'In that case we should get both desserts and taste each other's. But which one do you prefer?'

'I don't mind,' lied Chloe.

'Really? Well if you don't mind, then I'll take the chocolate, I just can't resist it. In fact, you see the double chocolate cake at the bottom there? I think I'll order that. It looks far more chocolatey.'

'You're being seriously sinful,' said Chloe, biting her lower lip in a mixture of anticipation and shame, 'but why not? You're absolutely right. Life is short and all that.'

16. Yet again I had lied [I was beginning to hear the sounds of cocks crowing in the kitchen]. I had been more or less allergic to chocolate all my life, but how could I have been honest about my desires in such a situation, where the love of chocolate had been so conclusively identified as an essential criterion of Chloe-compatibility?

17. Nevertheless, my lie was perverse, because of the assumptions it carried about my tastes and habits, namely that they were necessarily less valid than Chloe's and that she would be irretrievably offended by any divergence from her own. I might have made up a moving tale about myself and chocolate ['*I loved it more than anything in the world, but a panel of doctors warned me that I would die if I ate any more of it. I was in therapy for three years thereafter*'] and I might even have received ample sympathy from Chloe – but the risk was simply too high.

41

18.   My lie, as shameful as it was unavoidable, alerted me to a distinction between two kinds of lying, *lying in order to escape* and *lying in order to be loved*. Lies in seduction tend to be very different from lies in other areas. If I lie to the police about the speed at which I am stopped driving, I am doing so for a fairly straightforward motive, in order to escape a fine or an arrest. But lying in order to be loved carries with it the more perverse assumption that *if I do not lie, I cannot be loved*. It is an attitude that sees seductiveness as the emptying of all personal [and hence possibly diverging] characteristics, the true self being judged as irrevocably in conflict with [and hence unworthy of] the perfections found in the beloved.

19.   I had lied, but did Chloe like me any the more for it? Was she reaching over to take my hand or suggesting we should skip dessert [though that would perhaps have been asking too much] in order to head home? Certainly not, she merely expressed a certain disappointment, in view of the inferior taste of caramel, that I should have insisted so strongly on taking the chocolate, adding in an off-hand way that a chocophile was in the end perhaps as much of a problem as a chocophobe.

20.   Seduction is a form of acting, a move from spontaneous behaviour towards behaviour shaped by an audience. But just as an actor needs to have a concept of the audience's expecta-tions, so too the seducer must have an idea of what the beloved will want to hear — so that if there is a conclusive argument against lying in order to be loved, it is that the actor can have no idea of what his or her audience will be touched by. The only justification for acting would lie in its effectiveness com-

pared with spontaneity, but given the complexity of Chloe's character and doubts as to the attractions of mimetic behaviour, my chances of seducing Chloe could not have been significantly reduced by behaving either honestly or spontaneously. Inauthenticity seemed only to lead me into farcical somersaults of character and opinion.

21.   More often than not, we achieve our goals by coincidence rather than design, dispiriting news for the seducer, who is imbued with the spirit of positivism and rationalism, believing that with enough careful and almost scientific research, laws for the fall into love may be discovered. Seducers proceed in the hope of finding *love hooks* to ensnare the beloved – a certain smile, or opinion or way of holding a fork ... But it is an unfortunate fact that though love hooks exist for everyone; if we hit upon them in the course of seduction, it is more by chance than by calculation. After all, what had Chloe done to make me fall in love with her? My love for her had as much to do with the adorable way she had asked the waiter for some butter as it had with her sharing my views on the merits of Heidegger's *Being and Time*.

22.   Love hooks are marked by an extreme idiosyncrasy, apparently defying all logical causal laws. The positive steps I had sometimes seen women make to seduce me had rarely been the ones I had ended up being charmed by. I was prone to falling in love on account of completely tangential or incidental love hooks, ones the seducer had not been sufficiently aware of to push to the fore as valuable assets. I had once fallen in love with a woman who had a slight trace of down on her upper lip.

Normally squeamish about this, I had mysteriously been charmed by it in her case, my desire stubbornly deciding to collect there rather than around her warm smile, long blonde hair or intelligent conversation. When I discussed my attraction with friends, I struggled to suggest it had to do with an indefinable 'aura' she possessed – but I could not disguise the fact that I had fallen in love with nothing less than a hairy upper lip. When I saw the woman again, someone must have suggested electrolysis, for the down was gone, and [despite her many qualities] my desire soon followed suit.

23.　The Euston Road was still blocked with traffic when we made our way back towards Islington. Long before such questions could have become meaningful, it had been arranged that I would drop Chloe home, but nevertheless the dilemma of the seducer [*To kiss, or not to kiss*] remained a weighty presence in the car with us. At some point in seduction, the actor must risk losing his audience. The seducing self may attempt ingratiation by mimetic behaviour, but the game will eventually require one or other partner to define the situation, even at the risk of alienating the beloved in the process. A kiss would change everything, the contact of two skins would alter our position irrevocably, ending the coded speech and acknowledging the subtext. However, reaching the door of 23a Liverpool Road, awed by the dangers of misreading the signs, I concluded that the moment to propose a metaphorical cup of coffee had not yet arisen.

24.　But after such a tense and chocolate-rich meal, my stomach had suddenly developed quite different priorities, and I was forced to ask to be allowed up to the flat. I followed Chloe up the stairs, into the living room and was directed to the bathroom. Emerging a few minutes later with my intentions unaltered, I reached for my coat and announced to my love, with all the thoughtful authority of a man who has decided restraint would be best and fantasies entertained in weeks previous should remain just that, that I had spent a lovely evening, hoped to see her again soon, and would call her after the Christmas holidays. Pleased with such a mature farewell, I kissed her on both cheeks, wished her good-night and turned to leave the flat.

25.   Given the circumstances, it was fortunate that Chloe was not so easily persuaded, arresting my flight by the ends of my scarf. She drew me back into the apartment, placed both arms around me and, looking me firmly in the eye with a grin she had previously reserved for the idea of chocolate, whispered, *'We're not children, you know.'*

26.   And with these words, she placed her lips on mine and there began the longest and most beautiful kiss mankind has ever known.

CHAPTER FIVE

MIND AND BODY

1. Few things can be as antithetical to sex as thought. Sex is the product of the body, it is unreflective, Dionysiac and immediate, a release from rational bondage, an ecstatic resolution of physical desire. Next to it, thought appears nothing short of a sickness, a pathological urge to impose order, a symbol of the mind's melancholy inability to surrender to the flux. For me to have been thinking during sex was to have transgressed a fundamental law of intercourse, to have been guilty of a damning inability to preserve even this area for prelapsarian incogitance. But was there an alternative?

2. It was the sweetest kiss, everything one dreams a kiss might be. There was a light grazing, tender tentative forays that secreted the unique flavour of our skins, this before the pressure increased, before our lips parted then rejoined, mouths breathlessly articulating desire, my lips leaving Chloe's for a moment in order to run along her cheeks, her temples, her ears. She pressed her body closer to mine, our legs intertwined, dizzy, we collapsed on to the sofa, laughing, clutching at one another.

3. Yet if there was something interrupting this Eden, it was the mind, or rather, thought – the thought of how strange it

was for me to be lying in Chloe's living-room, passing my lips over hers, running my hands along her body, feeling her heat beside me. After all the ambiguity, the kiss had come so suddenly, so unexpectedly that my mind refused to cede control of events to the body. It was the thought of the kiss, rather than the kiss itself, that threatened to hold the attention.

4.   I could not help but think that a woman whose body had but a few hours ago been an area of complete privacy [only suggested by the outlines of her blouse and the contours of her skirt] was now preparing to reveal to me her innermost parts, long before [because of the age in which we happened to live] she had revealed the innermost parts of her soul. Though we had talked at length, I felt a disproportion between my day-time and night-time knowledge of Chloe, between the intimacy that contact with her sexual organs implied and the largely unknown dimensions of the rest of her life. But the presence of such thoughts, flowing in conjunction with our physical breathlessness, seemed to run rudely counter to the laws of desire, they seemed to be ushering in an unpleasant degree of objectivity, assuming the position of a third person in the room with us, one who would watch, observe, and perhaps even judge.

5.   'Wait,' said Chloe as I unbuttoned her blouse, 'I'm going to draw the curtains, I don't want the whole street to see. Or why don't we move into the bedroom? We'll have more space.'

We picked ourselves up from the cramped sofa and walked through the darkened apartment into Chloe's bedroom. A large white bed stood in the centre, piled high with cushions and papers, books and a telephone.

'Excuse the mess,' said Chloe, 'the rest of the flat's just for show, this is where I really live.'

There was an animal on top of all those cushions.

'Meet Guppy – my first love,' said Chloe, handing me a furry grey elephant whose face bore no signs of jealousy.

6.   There was a curious awkwardness while she cleared the surface of the bed, the eagerness of our bodies only a minute before had given way to a heavy silence that indicated how uncomfortably close we were to our own nakedness.

7.   Therefore, when Chloe and I undressed one another on top of the large white bed and, by the light of a small bedside lamp, saw each other's naked bodies for the first time, we attempted to be as unselfconscious about them as Adam and Eve before the Fall. I slipped my hands under Chloe's skirt and she unbuttoned my trousers with an air of breezy normality, as though it were no surprise for us to be laying eyes on the fascinating distinctiveness of each other's sexual organs. We had entered the phase where the mind must cede control to the body, where the mind must be cleared of all thought save the thought of passion, where there should be no room for judgement, nothing but desire.

8.   But if there was one thing likely to check our thought-less passion, it was our omnipresent clumsiness. It was clumsiness that was there to remind Chloe and me of the humour and bizarreness of ending up in bed together, I struggling rather awkwardly to peel off Chloe's underwear [some of it had

become caught around her knees], she having trouble with the buttons of my shirt – yet each of us trying not to comment, not to smile even, looking at one another with an earnest air of passionate desire, as though we had not noticed the potentially comic side of what was going on, sitting semi-naked on the edge of the bed, our faces flushed like those of guilty school-children.

9.   In retrospect, clumsiness in bed appears comic, almost farcical. Yet in the act itself, it is a minor tragedy, an unwelcome interruption to the smooth and direct flow of ardent embraces. The myth of passionate love making suggests it should be free of minor impediments such as getting bracelets caught, or cramps in one's leg, or hurting the partner in the effort to maximize their pleasure. The business of untangling hair or limbs forces an embarrassing degree of reason where only appetite should dwell.

10.   If the mind has traditionally been condemned, it is for its refusal to surrender control to causes supposedly beyond analysis; the philosopher in the bedroom is as ludicrous a figure as the philosopher in the nightclub. In both cases, the body is predominant and vulnerable, so that the mind becomes an instrument of silent, uninvolved judgement. Thought's infidelity lies in its privacy – '*If there is something that you cannot say to me,*' asks the lover, '*things that you must think alone, then am I truly in your heart?*' It is the resentment of this distance and superiority of thought that tarnishes the intellectual, the enemy not just of the lover, but of the nation, the cause and the class struggle.

11.   In the traditional dualism, the thinker and lover lie at opposite ends of the spectrum. The thinker *thinks* of love, the lover simply loves. I was not thinking anything cruel while I ran my hands and lips across Chloe's body, it was simply that Chloe would probably have been disturbed by the news I was thinking at all. Because thought implies judgement [and because we are all paranoid enough to take judgement to be negative], it is always suspect in the bedroom, where nakedness lays us open to every vulnerability. The range of complexes focused on the dimensions, colours, smells, and behaviour of sexual organs means that all trace of evaluative judgement must be banished. Hence the sighing that drowns the sounds of lovers' thoughts, a sighing that confirms the message, *I am too passionate to be thinking*. I kiss, and therefore I do not think – such is the official myth under which love making takes place, the bedroom a privileged space in which partners tacitly agree not to remind one another of the awe-inspiring wonder of their nudity.

12.   Humans have a unique ability to split in two and both act and stand back to watch themselves acting – and it is out of this division that reflexivity emerges. But the sickness that is excessive self-consciousness lies in an inability ever to fuse together the separation of viewer and viewed, the inability ever to engage in an activity and at the same time forget one is engaged in it. It is like the cartoon character who quite happily runs off a cliff and does not fall until the moment when he becomes self-conscious that there is no ground beneath him – at which point he shoots down to his death. How lucky the spontaneous person appears next to the self-conscious one, free as they are of the subject/object separation and of the lingering sense of a

mirror or third eye forever questioning, evaluating or simply watching what the central self [kissing Chloe's earlobe] is doing.

13.   There is the story of a nineteenth-century pious young virgin who, on the day of her wedding is warned by her mother, *'Tonight, it will seem your husband has gone mad, but you will find he has recovered by morning.'* Is the mind not offensive precisely because it symbolizes the refusal of this necessary insanity, keeping one's head while others are losing their breath?

14.   In the course of what Masters and Johnson have called a plateau period, Chloe looked up at me and asked, 'What are you thinking about, Socrates?'

'Nothing,' I answered.

'Bullshit, I can see it in your eyes, what are you smiling about?'

'Nothing, I tell you, or else everything, a thousand things; you, the evening, how we ended up here, how strange and yet comfortable it feels.'

'Strange?'

'I don't know, yes, strange, I suppose I'm being childishly self-conscious about things.'

Chloe smiled.

'What's so funny?'

'Turn round for a second.'

'Why?'

'Just turn over.'

On one side of the room, positioned over a chest of drawers and angled so it had been in Chloe's field of vision, was a large mirror that showed both of our bodies lying together, entangled in the bed linen. Had Chloe been watching us all the while?

'I'm sorry, I should have told you, it's just I didn't want to ask, not on the first night, you might have been shocked. But take a look, it doubles the pleasure.'

15.   Chloe drew me down towards her, parted her legs, and we gently resumed our rocking motions. I looked over to the side of the room, and in the mirror caught sight of two people, enlaced in sheets and in each other's arms, making love together on a bed. It was a moment before I could recognize the image in the mirror as that of Chloe and me. There was an initial discrepancy between the mirror and the reality of our actions, between the viewer and the viewed, but this was an enjoyable difference, not the crippling distance of subject and object that self-consciousness might sometimes imply. The mirror came to objectify what Chloe and I were doing, and in the process delivered me the thrill of being both actor and audience to our love making. The mind collaborated with the body, aroused at composing the erotic image of a man [his partner's legs now on top of his shoulders] making love to a woman.

16.   The mind can never leave the body, and to suggest it should is naïve. For to think does not always mean simply to judge [or not to feel], it is to leave one's own sphere, *to think of another*, to empathize, to place oneself where one's body is not, to become the other's body, to feel their pleasure and respond to their pulses, to climax with and for them. Without the mind, the body can think only of itself and its own pleasure, there can

be no synchronicity or search for the other's erogenous pathways. What one does not feel oneself, one must think. It is the mind that introduces congruence, and regulates pulses. Were the body allowed to run its course, there would be only insanity on one side and a frightened pious virgin on the other.

17. While ·it seemed as though Chloe and I were simply following our desire, there was a complex process of regulation and adjustment in play. The discrepancy between the technical and rational efforts to achieve simultaneity and the physical abandonment embodied in orgasm might have appeared ironic, but only from the modern perspective that love making should have been a matter solely for the body – and hence for nature.

18. A contradiction fouls the idea of the natural, for the myth of nature [like Hegel's Owl of Minerva] arrived only when it no longer existed, embodying a nostalgia for primitivism and sublimated mourning for lost energy. In an unspontaneous world obsessed with spontaneity, the sexologist calls in vain for the orgasm to reaffirm humanity's connections to a now deodorized wilderness, but is unable to induce it save through frustrated, bureaucratic syntax. [*The Joy of Sex*,[1] an enduring document of pleasure fascism, soberly and with some grammatical brio advises readers that:

'for preparation as well as orgasm, the flat of the hand on the vulva with the middle finger between the lips, and its tip moving in and out of the vagina, while the ball of the

[1] *The Joy of Sex, A gourmet guide to Lovemaking*, Alex Comfort, Quartet Books, 1989

palm presses hard just above the pubis, is probably the best method.']

19.   The rhythmic tempo on which Chloe and I had embarked was soon to reach its climax. A generous moisture lubricated our loins, our hair was wet with perspiration, we looked at one another with abandonment, mind and body united here as they would be in that other death [where prudes of a different kind have long sought divorce]. It would be a space beyond recorded time, compressed yet expansive, kaleidoscopic, polymorphous, supremely mortal, the disintegration of all syntax and law, the corset of language burst in screams beyond meaning, beyond the political, beyond the taboo, and into the realm of fluid forgetting.

CHAPTER SIX

MARXISM

1.   When we look at someone [an angel] from a position of unrequited love and imagine the pleasures that being in heaven with them might bring us, we are prone to overlook one important danger: how soon their attractions might pale if they began to love us back. We fall in love because we long to escape from ourselves with someone as beautiful, intelligent and witty as we are ugly, stupid and dull. But what if such a perfect being should one day turn around and decide they will love us back? We can only be somewhat shocked – how can they be as wonderful as we had hoped when they have the bad taste to approve of someone like us? If in order to love, we must believe that the beloved surpasses us in some way, does not a cruel paradox emerge when they return that love? We are led to ask, *'If s/he really is so wonderful, how is it possible that s/he could love someone like me?'*

2.   There is no richer territory for students of human psychology than that of the morning after. But Chloe had other priorities upon stumbling out of sleep: she had gone to wash her hair in the bathroom next door and I awoke to hear the sound of water crashing on tiles. I remained in bed, encasing myself in the shape and smell of her body that lingered in the

sheets. It was Saturday morning, and the first rays of the December sun were piercing through the curtains. I surveyed the room in privacy, thegover as voyeur, the lover as the anthropologist of the beloved, enchanted by her every cultural manifestation. It was a privilege to be curled up in her inner sanctum, in her bed, her sheets, looking at the objects that made up her daily life, at the walls she woke to every morning, at her alarm clock, a packet of aspirins, her watch and earrings on the bedside table. Love manifested itself as interest, fascination for everything Chloe owned, for the material signs of a life I had yet to discover but that seemed infinitely rich, full of the wonder the everyday takes on in the hands of the extraordinary. There was a bright yellow radio in one corner, a print by Matisse was leaning against a chair, her clothes from the night before were hanging in the closet by the mirror. On the chest of drawers there was a pile of paperbacks, next to it, her handbag and keys, a bottle of mineral water, and Guppy the elephant. By a form of cathexis, I fell in love with everything she owned, it all seemed so perfect, tasteful, different from what one could ordinarily buy in the shops [though I had seen the same radio just recently on Oxford Street]. The objects became fetishized, both displaced symbol and erotic substitute for my hair-washing mermaid next door.

3.   'Have you been trying on my underwear?' asked Chloe a moment later, emerging from the bathroom wrapped in a fluffy white robe and a towel around her head. 'What have you been doing all this time? You'll have to get out of bed now, because I've got to make it.'

I stirred, sighed, oohed and aahed.

'I'm going to go and prepare some breakfast, why don't you have a shower in the mean time. There's some clean towels in the closet. And how about a kiss?'

4.   The bathroom was another chamber of wonders, full of jars, lotions, potions, perfumes, the shrine of her body, my visit a watery pilgrimage. I washed my hair, sang like a hyena beneath the cascade, dried myself, and made use of a new toothbrush Chloe had given me. When I returned to the bedroom some fifteen minutes later, she was gone, the bed was made, the room tidied and the curtains opened.

5.   Chloe had not just gone and made toast, she'd prepared a breakfast feast. There was a basket of croissants, orange juice, a pot of fresh coffee, some eggs and toast, and a huge bowl of yellow and red flowers in the centre of the table.

6.   'It's fantastic,' I said, 'you prepared all this in the time it took me to have a shower and get dressed.'

'That's because I'm not lazy like you. Come on, let's eat before everything gets cold.'

'You're so sweet to have done this.'

'Rubbish.'

'No seriously, you are. It's not every day I get breakfast cooked for me,' I said, and put my arms around her waist.

She did not turn to look at me, but took my hand in hers and squeezed it for a moment.

'Don't flatter yourself, it's not for you I did this, I eat like this every weekend.'

I knew she was lying. She took a certain pride in mocking

57

the romantic, in being unsentimental, matter of fact, stoic, yet at heart, she was the complete opposite, idealistic, dreamy, giving, and deeply attached to everything she liked verbally to dismiss as *mushy*.

7.   In the course of a wonderful, *mushy* breakfast, I realized something that might perhaps have seemed glaringly obvious, but that struck me as both unexpected and most complicated – that Chloe had begun to feel for me a little of what I had long felt for her. Objectively, it was not an unusual thought, but in falling in love with her, I had somehow completely overlooked the possibility of reciprocation. It was not necessarily unwelcome, I had simply not taken it into account, I had counted more on loving than being loved. And if I had concentrated largely on the former emotion, it was perhaps because being loved is always the more complicated of the two, Cupid's arrow easier to send than receive, to give than accept.

8.   It was this difficulty of receiving that struck me over breakfast, for though the croissants could not have been more French and the coffee more aromatic, something about the attention and affection they symbolized disturbed me. Chloe had opened her body to me the night before, in the morning she had opened her kitchen, but I could not now prevent a sense of uneasiness [that might even have bordered on irritation] amounting to the muffled thought, '*What have I done to deserve this?*'

9.   Few things can be at once so exhilarating and so terrifying as to recognize that one is the object of another's love, for if

one is not wholly convinced of one's own loveability, then receiving affection may feel like being given a great honour without quite knowing what one has done to earn it. However much I was myself in love with Chloe, her attentions were proving somewhat unnerving. There are people for whom such demonstrations are only a confirmation of what they have suspected all along – that they are inherently lovable. Then there are those who, lacking a belief in their own loveability, are not quite so easily convinced. Lovers unfortunate enough to prepare breakfast for such a type must brace themselves for the recriminations due to all false flatterers.

10.　What arguments are about is never as important as the discomfort for which they are an excuse. Ours started over strawberry jam.

　　'Do you have any strawberry jam?' I asked Chloe, surveying the laden table.

　　'No, but there's raspberry here, do you mind?'

　　'Sort of, yes.'

　　'Well, there's blackberry as well.'

　　'I hate blackberry, do you like blackberry?'

　　'Yeah, why not?'

　　'It's horrible. So there's no decent jam?'

　　'I wouldn't put it quite like that. There are five pots of jam on the table, there's just no strawberry.'

　　'I see.'

　　'Why are you making such a big deal of it?'

　　'Because I hate having breakfast without decent jam.'

　　'But there is decent jam, just not the one you like.'

　　'Is the shop far?'

'Why?'

'I am going out to buy some.'

'For Christ's sake, we've just sat down, everything will be cold if you go now.'

'I'll go.'

'Why, if everything's going to get cold?'

'Because I need jam, that's why.'

'What's up with you?'

'Nothing, why?'

'You're being ridiculous.'

'No, I'm not.'

'Yes, you are.'

'I just need jam.'

'Why are you being so impossible? I've cooked you this whole breakfast and all you can do is make a fuss about some pot of jam. If you really want your jam, just get the hell out of here and eat it in someone else's company.'

11.   There was a silence, Chloe's eyes glazed, then abruptly she stood up and walked into the bedroom, slamming the door behind her. I remained at the table, listening to what might have been crying, feeling like the idiot I was for upsetting the woman I claimed to love.

12.   Unrequited love may be painful, but it is safely painful, because it does not involve inflicting damage on anyone but oneself, a private pain that is as bitter-sweet as it is self-induced. But as soon as love is reciprocated, one must be prepared to give up the passivity of simply *being* hurt and take on the responsibility of perpetrating hurt oneself.

13.   But responsibility can be the greatest burden. The repugnance I felt towards myself for hurting Chloe was momentarily turned against her. I hated her for all the efforts she had made with me, for her weakness in believing in me, for her bad taste in allowing me to upset her. It suddenly seemed overly sentimental, almost pathetic, that she had given me her toothbrush, prepared breakfast for me, and begun to cry in the bedroom like a child. I hated this sensitivity that she had developed towards me and my moods, and was overcome by an urge to punish her for such weakness.

14.   What had turned me into such a monster? The fact that I had always been something of a Marxist.

15.   There is the old joke made by the Marx who laughed about not deigning to belong to a club that would accept someone like him as a member – a truth as appropriate in love as it is in club membership. We laugh at the Marxist position because of its absurd contradiction:

> How is it possible that I should both wish to join a club, and yet lose that wish as soon as it comes true?

> How was it that I might have wished Chloe to love me, but be irritated by her when she did so?

16.   Perhaps because the origins of a certain kind of love lie in an impulse to escape ourselves and our weaknesses by an amorous alliance with the beautiful or the powerful – God, the club, Her/Him. But if the beloved loves us back [if God answers our prayer,

if membership is extended], we are forced to return to ourselves, and are hence reminded of the things that had driven us into love in the first place. Perhaps it was not love we wanted after all, perhaps it was simply someone in whom to believe, but how can we continue to believe in the beloved now that they believe in us?

17.   I wondered how Chloe could be justified in even thinking she could base her emotional life around a scoundrel like me. If she appeared to be a little in love, was it not simply because she had misunderstood me? It was the classic Marxist thought, where love is desired, but impossible to accept, for fear of the disappointment that will ensue when the true self is revealed – a disappointment that has normally already occurred [perhaps at the hands of a parent] but is now projected on to the future. Marxists feel their core self to be so deeply unacceptable that intimacy will necessarily reveal them to be charlatans. Therefore why accept the gift of love, when it is sure to be taken away imminently? *If you love me now, this is only because you are not seeing the whole of me*, thinks the Marxist, *and if you're not seeing the whole of me, it would be crazy to grow used to your love until such time as you do*.

18.   An orthodox Marxist alliance will for these reasons be founded and depend on an unequal exchange of affect. Though from a position of unrequited love, they long to see their love returned, Marxists would unconsciously prefer that their dreams remain in the realm of fantasy. They would prefer that their love was not much more than acknowledged, that their partner not call them too often, or do them the decency of being emotionally unavailable the majority of the time, a situation in accordance with their sense of worth – *why should others think any better of*

them than they think of themselves? If the beloved by some accident should think rather well of them [should sleep with them, smile at them and get them breakfast], then the Marxist's first impulse may be to shatter the idyll, *not because it is unwelcome, but because it feels undeserved.* Only so long as the loved one believes the Marxist is more or less nothing can the Marxist continue to believe that the loved one is more or less everything. For the beloved to begin loving would directly tarnish their perfections by an unfortunate association with scoundrels. If Chloe had been lowered in my esteem by sleeping with and being nice to me, was it not perhaps because she had in the process caught *I-infection*, infected by dangerous proximity to a Marxist?

19.   I had often seen Marxism at work in others. At the age of sixteen, I was for a while in love with a fifteen-year-old girl, who was both captain of her school volleyball team, very beautiful and a committed Marxist.

'If a man says he'll call me at nine,' she once told me over a glass of orange squash that I bought for her at the school cafeteria, 'and he does actually ring at nine, I'll refuse to take the call. After all, what's he so desperate for? The only guy I like is the one who'll keep me waiting, by nine thirty I'll do anything for him.'

I must at that age have had an intuitive understanding of her Marxism, for I remember efforts to seem uninterested in anything she said or did. My reward came with our first kiss a few weeks later, but though she was unquestionably beautiful [and as adept at the arts of love as she was at volleyball], the relationship did not last. I found it simply too tiring to make a point of always calling late.

20.   A few years later, I was seeing another girl, who [like a good Marxist] believed that men should in some way defy her in order to earn her love. One morning, before going out for a walk with her in the park, I had put on an old and particularly revolting electric blue pullover.

'Well one thing is for sure, I'm not going out with you looking like that,' exclaimed Sophie when she saw me coming down the stairs, 'You've got to be joking if you think I'll be seen with someone with that kind of jumper on.'

'Sophie, what does it matter what I'm wearing? We're only going for a walk in the park,' I replied, half-fearing that she might have meant what she said.

'I don't care where we're going, I tell you, I'm not going to the park with you unless you change.'

But pig-headedness descended on me and I refused to do as Sophie wanted, arguing the case of the electric jumper with such force that a while later we headed for the Royal Hospital Gardens with the offending garment still in place. When we reached the gates of the park, Sophie, who had till then been in a mild sulk, suddenly broke the silence, took my arm, gave me a kiss and said in words that perhaps provide us with the essence of Marxism, 'Don't worry, I'm not angry with you, I'm glad you kept the old horror on, *I would have thought you were so weak if you'd done what I told you.*'

21.   The Marxist cry is hence a paradoxical, '*Defy me and I will love you, don't call me on time, and I will kiss you, don't sleep with me and I will adore you.*' Expressed in its horticultural form, Marxism is the complex that involves thinking the grass is always greener on the other side. Alone in our garden, we

gaze covetously at the neighbour's green patch [or at Chloe's beautiful eyes or the way she combed her hair]. The point is not that the neighbour's patch is in itself any greener or lusher than our own [that Chloe's eyes were necessarily any nicer than the next person's or that the same comb from the same chemist could not do the same trick on anyone's hair]. What makes the grass greener and desirable is that it is not ours, that it belongs to the neighbour, that it is not tainted with *I-infection*.

22.   But what if the neighbour were suddenly to fall in love with us, and apply for permission from the council to break down the wall separating the two gardens? Would it not threaten our herbivorous envy? Would not the neighbour's patch slowly lose its appeal and begin to look as tired and worn as our own lawn? Perhaps what we were looking for was not necessarily greener grass, but grass that we could admire [whatever its condition] *because it was not our own*.

23.   To be loved by someone is to realize how much they share in the same dependent needs the resolution of which had attracted us to them in the first place. We would not love if there were no lack within us, but paradoxically, we are offended by a similar lack in the other. Expecting to find the answer, we find only the duplicate of our own problem. We realize how much they too need to find an idol, we see that the beloved does not escape our sense of helplessness, and are hence forced to give up on the childish passivity of hiding behind Godlike admiration and worship, in order to take on the responsibility of both carrying and being carried.

24.   Albert Camus suggested we fall in love with people because, from the outside, they look so *whole*, both physically whole and emotionally 'together', when subjectively we feel so dispersed and confused. Lacking a coherent narrative, a stable personality, a fixed direction, a thematic unity, we hallucinate such qualities in the other. Was there not something of this in my relationship with Chloe, namely that from the outside [prior to epidermal contact], she seemed wonderfully controlled, possessed of a distinct and continuous character [see fig 6.1], whereas post-coitally I saw her as vulnerable, prone to collapse, dispersed, needy? Was this not a case of a Nietzschean self, the mere sum of its actions, attached and sexually attracted to the idea of Bishop Butler's 'essential' self? Therefore the echo of Bob Dylan's celebrated *'Don't fall apart on me [tonight]'* after the tears had flowed.

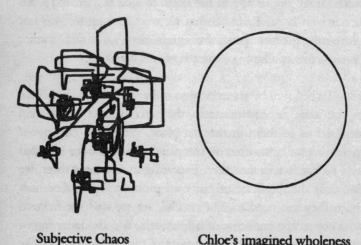

Subjective Chaos   Chloe's imagined wholeness

Figure 6.1

25. The desired person must therefore achieve the correct balance for the Marxist in an area where imbalance seems the norm, the balance between excessive vulnerability and excessive independence. Chloe's tears had frightened me because they had acted as an unconscious reminder of my own sensitivity towards her. I had condemned in her a dependence I feared in myself. Yet whatever the problems of vulnerability, I knew that independence could be as much of a problem, having witnessed women whose haughty coldness almost negated the need for a lover. Chloe had a difficult task: to be not so vulnerable as to endanger my independence, but not so independent as to deny my vulnerability.

26. There is a long and gloomy tradition in Western thought arguing that love can ultimately only be thought of as an unreciprocated, admiring, Marxist exercise, where desire thrives on the impossibility of ever seeing love returned. According to this view, love is simply a direction, not a place, and burns itself out with the attainment of its goal, the possession [in bed or otherwise] of the loved one. The whole of Troubadour poetry of twelfth-century Provence was based on coital delay, the poet repeating his plaints to a woman who repeatedly declined the desperate man's offers. Four centuries later, Montaigne had the same idea of what made love grow when he declared that: 'In love, there is nothing but a frantic desire for what flees from us' – a view echoed by Anatole France's maxim: 'It is not customary to love what one has.' Stendhal believed love could be brought about only on the basis of fear of losing the loved one, Denis de Rougemont argued, 'The most serious obstruction is the one

preferred above all. It is the one most suited to intensifying passion,' and Roland Barthes limited desire to a longing for what was by definition unattainable.

27.   According to this view, lovers cannot do anything save oscillate between the twin poles of *yearning for* and *annoyance with*. Love has no middle ground, it is simply a direction, what it desires it cannot desire beyond capture. Love should therefore burn itself out with its fulfilment, possession of the desired extinguishes desire. There was a danger that Chloe and I would trap ourselves in just such a Marxist spiral, where one person's increasing love would prompt an ever decreasing love in the other until love would be spiralled into oblivion.

28.   A happier resolution emerged. I returned home from the breakfast guilty, shame-faced, apologetic and ready to do anything to win Chloe back. It was not easy [she hung up on me at first, then asked me whether I made a point of behaving like a 'small-time suburban punk' with women I had slept with], but after apologies, insults, laughter and tears, Romeo and Juliet were to be seen together later that afternoon, mushily holding hands in the dark at a four thirty screening of *Love and Death* at the National Film Theatre. Happy endings, for now at least.

29.   There is usually a Marxist moment in most relationships [the moment when it becomes clear that love is reciprocated] and the way it is resolved depends on the balance between self-love and self-hatred. If self-hatred gains the upper hand, then the one who has received love will declare that the beloved [on

some excuse or other] is not good enough for them [not good enough by virtue of association with no-goods]. But if self-love gains the upper hand, both partners may accept that seeing their love reciprocated is not proof of how low the beloved is, but of how lovable they have themselves turned out to be.

CHAPTER SEVEN

FALSE NOTES

1.   Long before we've had the chance to become familiar with our loved one, we may be filled with the curious sense that we know them already. It seems as though we've met them somewhere before, in a previous life perhaps, or in our dreams. In Plato's *Symposium*, Aristophanes explains this feeling of familiarity with the claim that the loved one was our long lost 'other half' whose body we had originally been stuck to. In the beginning, all human beings were hermaphrodites with double backs and flanks, four hands and four legs and two faces turned in opposite directions on the same head. These hermaphrodites were so powerful and their pride so overweening that Zeus was forced to cut them in two, into a male and female half – and from that day, each man and each woman has yearned to rejoin the half from which he or she has been severed.

2.   Chloe and I spent Christmas apart, but when we returned to London in the new year, we began spending every available minute in each other's company, mostly in each other's arms, often in each other's beds. We led the typical romance of late twentieth-century urban life, sandwiched between office hours [the phone as umbilical cord when the waiting grew unbear-

able], animated by such external movements as walks in the park, strolls through bookshops and meals in restaurants. These first weeks were akin to rediscovering the other half of an original hermaphrodite body. Agreement was found on so many different issues, we were forced to conclude that, despite an absence of clear separation marks, we must once have been two parts of the same body.

3.   When philosophers imagine Utopian societies, they rarely envisage them as melting pots of difference, rather these societies are based around like-mindedness and unity, similarity and homogeneity, a set of common goals and assumptions. It was precisely this congruence that made life with Chloe so attractive, the fact that after endless irreconcilable differences in matters of the heart, I had at last found someone whose jokes I understood without the need of a dictionary, whose views seemed miraculously close to mine, whose loves and hates kept tandem with my own and with whom I repeatedly found myself saying, *It's amazing, I was about to say/think/do/tell the same thing . . .*

4.   Critics of love have been rightly suspicious of fusion, the belief that differences between people can be so erased that two blend into one. Suspicion stems from the sense that it is easier to assume similarity than difference [what is familiar does not have to be *invented*], and that in the absence of evidence to the contrary, we will always invent what we know, rather than what we don't and fear. We base our fall into love upon insufficient material, and supplement our ignorance with desire. But, as the critics point out, time will show us that the skin separating our

bodies is not just a physical boundary, but representative of deeper, psychological contradictions one would be foolish to try to transcend.

5.   Therefore, in the mature account of love, one does not fall at first sight. Falling comes only when one knows how deep the waters are into which to plunge. Only after much exchange of early history, opinions on politics, art, science and what they like to have for dinner should two people decide they are ready to love one another, a decision taken on the basis of mutual understanding and confirmed rather than imagined affinity. In the mature account of love, it is only when one truly knows one's partner that love is given a chance to grow. And yet in the perverse reality of love [love that is born precisely *before* we know] increased knowledge may be as much a hurdle as an inducement – for it may bring Utopia into dangerous conflict with reality.

6.   I date the realization that, whatever charming similarities we had identified between us, Chloe was perhaps not the person from whom Zeus's cruel stroke had severed me, to a moment somewhere in the middle of March when she introduced me to a new pair of her shoes. It was perhaps a pedantic matter over which to make such a decision, but shoes were an important symbol of aesthetic, and hence by extension psychological, difference. I had often noticed how certain areas and coverings of the body could say more about a person than others: how shoes suggested more than pullovers, thumbs more than elbows, underwear more than overcoats, ankles more than shoulders.

72

7.   What was wrong with Chloe's shoes? Objectively speaking, nothing [but when did one ever fall in love *objectively*?]. She had bought them one Saturday morning in a shop on the King's Road, ready for a party we were invited to that evening. I understood the blend of high- and low-heeled shoe that the designer had tried to incorporate; the platformed sole rising sharply up to a heel with the breadth of a flat shoe but as tall as a stiletto. Then there was the high, faintly rococo collar, decorated with a bow, stars, and framed by a piece of chunky ribbon. The shoes were the height of fashion, they were well made, they were clean – yet they were precisely the kind of shoes I hated.

8.   'Don't you just love them?' Chloe had asked rhetorically, full of the excitement of a new purchase, 'I'm going to wear them every day, don't you think they're terrific?'

But though I loved her, the magic wand that might have transformed them into objects of desire remained impotent to perform its usual alchemy.

'I tell you, I could have bought the whole shop. They've got such great things there. You should have seen the boots they had.'

I was shocked to see Chloe [with whom I had agreed on almost everything till then] fall into raptures over what I took to be at best a most unattractive pair of shoes. My idea of who she was, my Aristophanic *certainty* of who she was, had not included this particular enthusiasm. Disturbed by the thought of what Chloe had had in mind when she bought them, I asked myself, 'How could she like both this kind of shoe *and* me?'

9.   Chloe's choice of shoe was an uncomfortable reminder that she existed in her own right [beyond fusional fantasies], that her tastes were not always my own, and that however compatible we might be over certain things, compatibility did not extend indefinitely. It was a reminder that getting to know someone is not always the pleasant process that common sense makes it out to be, for just as one may strike on delightful similarities, one may also encounter threatening differences. Staring down at Chloe's shoes, I became aware of a fleeting desire *not* to get to know certain things about her, lest they jar with the beautiful image that, almost from the moment I had first laid eyes on her, I had built up in my imagination.

10.   Baudelaire wrote a prose poem about a man who spends a day walking around Paris with a woman he feels ready to love. Because they agree on so many things, by evening, he is sure he has found the perfect companion with whose soul his own may unite. Thirsty, they go to a glamorous new café on the corner of a boulevard, where the man notices the arrival of an impoverished, working-class family who have come to gaze through the plate-glass window of the café at the elegant guests, dazzling white walls and gold trimmings. The eyes of these poor on-lookers are full of wonder at the display of wealth and beauty inside, filling the narrator with pity and shame at his privileged position. He turns to look at his loved one in the hope of seeing his thoughts reflected in her eyes. But the woman with whose soul he was prepared to unite snaps that these wretches with their wide, gaping eyes are unbearable to her and asks him to tell the owner to have them moved on straightaway. Does not every love story have these moments? A

search for eyes that will reflect one's thoughts and that ends up with a [tragi-comic] divergence – be it over the class struggle or a pair of shoes.

11.   Perhaps it is true that the easiest people to fall in love with are those who tell us very little about themselves beyond what we can read from their face or voice. In fantasy, a person is endlessly, *love*-ably malleable. If one is feeling suitably dreamy, there is nothing as romantic as the love stories one writes for oneself on long train journeys, staring at an attractive person gazing out of the window – a perfect love story interrupted when Troilus or Criseyde looks back inside the carriage and starts up a dull conversation with their neighbour or blows their nose unappealingly into a dirty handkerchief.

12.   The dismay that greater acquaintance with the beloved can bring is like composing a wonderful symphony in one's head and later hearing it played in a concert hall by a full orchestra. Though we are impressed to hear so many of our ideas confirmed in performance, we cannot help but notice tiny things that are not quite as we had intended them to be. Is one of the violinists not a little off key? Is the flute not a little late coming in? Is the percussion not a little too loud? People we love at first sight are as wonderful as a symphony composed in one's head. They are as free from conflicting tastes in shoes or literature as the unrehearsed symphony is free from off-key violins or late flutes. But as soon as the fantasy is played out in a concert hall, the angelic beings who floated through consciousness come down to earth and reveal themselves as material beings, laden with their own [often awkward] mental and

physical history – we learn they use a certain kind of toothpaste, and have a certain way of clipping their toe nails and prefer Beethoven to Bach and pencils to fountain-pens.

13.   Chloe's shoes were only one of a number of false notes detected in the early period of the relationship, the period of transition [if ever one can talk so optimistically] between inner fantasy and outer reality. Living day to day with her was like acclimatizing myself to a foreign country, and being prey therefore to occasional xenophobia at departures from my own traditions and history. It implied a geographic and cultural dislocation, forcing us to cross an exposed period between two habits, that of living alone and that of living together, a period when [for instance] Chloe's occasional late-night enthusiasm for a nightclub or mine for an avant-garde film risked running counter to the other's established nocturnal or cinematic customs.

14.   Threatening differences did not collect at the major points [nationality, gender, class, occupation], but rather at the little junctures of taste and opinion. Why did Chloe insist on leaving the pasta to boil for those fatal extra minutes? Why was I so attached to my current pair of glasses? Why did she have to do her gym exercises in the bedroom every morning? Why did I always need eight hours' sleep? Why did she not have more time for opera? Why did I not have more time for Joni Mitchell? Why did she hate seafood so much? How could one explain my resistance to flowers and gardening? Or hers to trips over water? How come she liked to keep her options open about God ['*at least till the first cancer*']? But why was I so closed on the matter?

15.   Anthropologists tell us that the group always comes before the individual, that to understand the latter, one must pass through the former, be it nation, tribe, clan or family. Chloe had no great fondness for her family, but when her parents invited us to spend Sunday with them at their home near Marlborough, I begged her to take up the offer. 'You'll see, you'll hate it,' she said, 'but if you really want to, all right. You'll at least understand the things I've been trying to run away from all my life.'

16.   Despite her desire for autonomy, witnessing Chloe in her home environment helped to explain certain sides to her, as well as the origin of some of our differences. Everything about Gnarled Oak Cottage was a sign that Chloe had been born in one world [one galaxy almost] and I another. The living room was decorated in imitation Chippendale furniture, the carpet was a stained reddish brown, dusty book cases with volumes of Trollope and Stubbs-esque paintings lined the walls, three salival dogs were running in and out between the living-room and the garden, a corpulent plant sagged in one corner. Chloe's mother wore a thick purple pullover with holes in it, a flowery baggy skirt, and long grey hair scraped back without design. One half expected to find bits of straw on her, an aura of rural nonchalance reinforced by her repeated forgettings of my name [and her creative approach to finding me another]. I thought of the difference between Chloe's mother and my own, the con-trasting introductions to the world that these two women had performed. However much Chloe had run away from all of this, to the big city, to her own values and friends, the family still

represented a common genetic and historical tradition to which she belonged. I noticed a cross-over between the generations: the mother preparing potatoes in the same way as Chloe, crushing a little garlic into the butter and grinding sea salt over them or sharing her daughter's enthusiasm for painting, or taste in Sunday papers. The father was a keen rambler, and Chloe loved walking too, often dragging me on weekends for a brisk tour of Hampstead Heath, proclaiming the benefits of fresh air in a way that her father had perhaps once done.

17.   It was all so strange and new. The house in which she had grown up evoked a whole past on which I had missed out, and which I would have to take on board in order to understand her. The meal was largely spent on a question–answer volley between Chloe and her parents on various aspects of family folklore: Had the insurance paid for Gran's hospital bills? Was the watertank mended? Had Carolyn heard from the estate agency yet? Was it true Lucy was going to study in the States? Had anyone read Aunt Sarah's novel? Was Henry really going to marry Jemima? [All these characters who had entered Chloe's life long before I had – and might, with the tenacity of everything familial, still be there when I was gone.]

18.   It was intriguing to see how different the parental perception of Chloe could be from my own. Whereas I had known her to be both accommodating and generous, at home she was known to be somewhat bossy and demanding. As a child she had been a mini-autocrat whom the parents had nicknamed Miss Pompadosso after the heroine of a children's book.

Whereas I had known Chloe to be level-headed about money and her career, the father remarked that his daughter 'did not understand the first thing about how things work in the real world', while the mother joked about her 'bullying all her boyfriends into submission'. I was forced to add to my understanding of Chloe a whole section of her reality prior to my arrival, my vision of her colliding with that imposed by the initial family narrative.

19.   In the afternoon, Chloe showed me around the house. She took me into the room at the top of the stairs into which she'd been afraid to go as a child, because her uncle had once told her a ghost lived inside the piano. We looked into her old bedroom that her mother now used as a studio, and she pointed out a hatch that she had used to get into the attic in order to escape with her elephant Guppy whenever she'd been miserable. We took a walk in the garden, past a still-bruised tree at the bottom of a slope into which the family car had ploughed when she had once dared her brother to take the handbrake off. She showed me the neighbours' house, whose blackberry bushes she had picked clean in the summers, and whose former owner's son she had kissed on the way back from school.

20.   Later in the afternoon, I took a walk in the garden with her father, a donnish man to whom thirty years of marriage had given some distinctive views on the subject.

'I know my daughter and you are fond of one another. I'm no expert on love, but I'll tell you something. In the end, I've found that it doesn't really matter who you marry. If you like them at the beginning, you probably won't like them at the end. And if you start off hating them, there's always the chance you'll end up thinking they're all right.'

21. On the train back to London that evening, I felt exhausted, weary at all the differences between Chloe's early world and mine. While the stories and settings of her past had enchanted me, they had also proved terrifying and bizarre, all these years and habits before I had known her, but that were as much a part of who she was as the shape of her nose or the colour of her eyes. I felt a primitive nostalgia for familiar surroundings, recognizing the disruption that every relationship entails – a whole new person to learn about, to suggest myself to, to acclimatize myself to. It was perhaps a moment of fear at the thought of all the differences I would find in Chloe, all the times she would be one thing, and I another, when our world views would be incapable of alignment. Staring out of the window at the Wiltshire countryside, I had a lost child's longing for someone I could already wholly understand, the eccentricities of whose house, parents and history I had already tamed.

CHAPTER EIGHT

LOVE OR LIBERALISM

1.   If I may be allowed to return for a moment to Chloe's shoes, I should mention that the revelation of their purchase did not end with my negative yet privately formulated analysis. I confess that it ended in the second greatest argument of our relationship, in tears, insults, shouting and the right shoe crashing through a pane of glass on to the pavement of Denbigh Street. The sheer melodramatic intensity of the event aside, the matter sustains philosophical interest because it symbolizes a choice as radical in the personal sphere as in the political: the choice between *love and liberalism*.

2.   The choice has often been missed in an optimistic equation of the two terms, one considered the epitome of the other. But if they have been linked, it is always in an implausible marriage, for it seems impossible to talk of love *and* letting live, and if we are left to live, we are not usually loved. We may well ask why the cruelty witnessed between lovers would not be tolerated [or even considered conceivable] beyond conditions of open enmity. Then, to build bridges between shoes and nations, we may ask related questions: why do the countries that have no language of community or citizenship leave their members isolated but unmolested? And why do the countries that talk

most of community, love and brotherhood routinely end up slaughtering great swathes of their populations?

3.   'Well? Do you like them then?' repeated Chloe.
      'Frankly, I don't.'
      'Why not?'
      'I just don't like that kind of shoe. It looks like a pelican.'
      'Really, but it's elegant.'
      'No, it's not.'
      'Yes it is, look at the heel, and the bow. They're great.'
      'You'll be pressed to find anyone to agree with you on that one.'
      'That's because you don't know anything about fashion.'
      'Maybe, but I know a horrible shoe when I see one.'
      'It's not *horrible*.'
      'Face it, Chloe, it *is* quite horrible.'
      'You're just jealous I bought a new pair of shoes.'
      'I'm just telling you what I feel. I really don't think they're suitable for the party tonight.'
      'That's great. That's why I bloody bought them.'
      'So wear them.'
      'How can I now?'
      'Well, why shouldn't you?'
      'Because a minute ago, you told me I looked like a pelican in them.'
      'You do.'
      'So you want me to go to a party looking like a pelican?'
      'Not particularly. That's why I'm telling you they're awful.'
      'Well, why can't you keep your opinions to yourself?'

'Because I care about you. *Someone* has to let you know when you've bought a disgusting pair of shoes. But why does it matter so much what I think anyway?'

'Because I want you to like them. I bought them hoping you'd like them, and now you tell me I'm going to look like an alien wearing them. Why does everything I do always have to be wrong?'

'Come on, don't throw that one at me. You know that isn't true.'

'Yes it is, you don't even like my shoes.'

'But I like almost everything else.'

'So why can't you just forget about the shoes?'

'Because you deserve better.'

4.   The reader can be spared the full melodrama, it suffices to say that moments later, and with the unexpectedness of a tornado, tempers flared, Chloe took off one of the offensive shoes [supposedly so as to let me look at it], and I chose to duck the incoming projectile, letting it [perhaps foolishly] crash through the glass behind me and fly down on to the street.

5.   Our argument was peppered with the paradoxes of love and liberalism. What did it really matter what Chloe's shoes were like? There were so many other wonderful sides to her, was it not rather spoiling the game to arrest my gaze on this one detail? Why could I not have politely lied to her as I might have lied to a friend? My only excuse lay in the claim that I loved her, that she was my ideal – save for the shoes – and that I therefore felt compelled to point out this little flaw, something I would never have done with a friend [whose departures from

my ideal would have been too numerous to begin with, a friendship in which the concept of an ideal would not have even entered into my thinking]. *Because I loved her, I told her* – therein lay my sole defence.

6.   In our more idealistic moments, we imagine romantic love to be akin to Christian love, a universal emotion that declares *I will love you for everything that you are,* a love that has no conditions, that draws no boundaries, that adores every last shoe, that is the embodiment of acceptance. But the arguments that hound lovers are a reminder that Christian love does not well survive the transition into the bedroom. Its message seems more suited to the universal than the particular, to the love of all men for all women, to the love of two neighbours who will not hear each other snoring.

7.   Romantic love cannot be virginal, it talks the language of a specific body, it is concerned with uniqueness, not generality. It is about falling in love with neighbour A because he or she has a smile or freckle or laugh or set of opinions or set of ankles neighbour B does not. Jesus side-stepped this thorny issue by refusing to index love to criteria, avoiding much of the cruelty of love in the process. For it is with criteria that love becomes painful, it is when we try to turn neighbour A into neighbour B, or turn neighbour B into the idealized B we imagined before marriage that shoes start to fly and divorces are filed. It is in this gap between the ideal we imagine and the reality time reveals, that impatience, perfectionism and finally intolerance, will breed.

8.   Though it was not always a matter for glaziers, illiberalism was never one sided. There were a thousand things about me that drove Chloe insane: why was I so often moody? Why did I insist on wearing a coat that looked a century old? Why did I always knock the duvet off the bed in my sleep? Why did I think Saul Bellow was such a great writer? Why had I not yet learnt how to park a car without leaving most of the wheel on the pavement? Why did I constantly put my feet on the bed? All this was very far from the love suggested by the New Testament, the kind of love that never comments on an ugly pair of shoes, a piece of salad between the teeth or a stubbornly held but false opinion on who wrote *The Rape of the Lock*. Yet all these were things that made up the domestic gulag, the daily attempt to tug the other closer to a given concept of how they should be. If we imagine ideal and reality as two partly overlapping circles, then it was the crescent of difference that through our arguments we tried to eliminate, making one circle of two.

Figure 8.1

9.   And what excuse was there for this? Nothing but the old line that all parents, military generals, Chicago school economists, and Communists will use before upsetting others – *I care about you, therefore I will upset you, I have honoured you with a vision of how you should be, therefore I will hurt you.*

10.   Chloe and I would never have allowed ourselves a comparable intensity of argument within friendship. A protective sheath separates friends, constructed out of a code of propriety and civility, a sheath of biological unfamiliarity that prevents the passage of hostile drives. But Chloe and I were no longer practising safe sex: something about sleeping and bathing together, watching each other brush our teeth or cry in front of a *mushy* movie had permitted the sheath between us to break, infecting us not just with love, but also with its flipside, abuse. We equated our knowledge of one another with a form of ownership and license: *I know you, therefore I own you.* It was no coincidence that in the chronology of our love, politeness [friendship] stopped after coitus, and our first argument flared over the breakfast table the next morning.

11.   The tearing of the sheath began a free-market exchange of previously monopolized goods, it began the expression of tension normally [charitably] left to operate within the bounds of self-criticism. To use Freudian language, we participated not simply in our own super-ego – ego conflicts [see fig 8.2], but also in each other's. When the cross-over was simply between ego A and ego B, there would be love: when it was super-ego A attacking ego B, shoes began to fly.

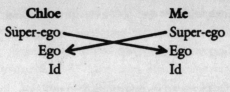

Figure 8.2

12.   Intolerance starts with two elements, a concept of what is right and wrong, and the idea that one cannot let others live without seeing the light. When Chloe and I started arguing one night about the films of Eric Rohmer [she hated them, I loved them], we forgot there was a chance Rohmer's films could be both good *and* bad depending on who was watching them. The argument reduced itself to an exercise in forcing the other person to accept one's point of view, rather than in our realizing the legitimacy of divergence. Similarly, my hatred of Chloe's shoes was not limited by a sense that though *I* might have disliked them, they were not inherently dislikable.

13.   It is this shift from the personal to the universal that is the tyrannical one, the moment when a personal judgement is universalized and made applicable to one's girlfriend or boy-friend [or all the citizens of a country], the moment when *I think this is good* becomes *I think this is good for you too*. Over certain things, both Chloe and I believed that we knew what was right, and that belief was deemed to allow us to instruct each other in universal truths. The tyrannical claim of love is to force a partner [supposedly out of love] into abandoning the

87

film they may wish to see, or shoes they may wish to buy, in order to accept what is [at best] only a personal judgement, masquerading as universal truth.

14.   Politics seems an incongruous field to link to love, but can we not read, in the blood-stained history of the French Revolution or of the Fascist and Communist experiments, something of the same amorous structure? Is there not the same ideal set against a diverging reality, producing an impatience [the impatience of the axe-man] with the crescent of difference? Amorous politics begins its infamous history in the course of the French Revolution, when it was first proposed [with all the choice of a rape] that the state would not just govern but also *love* its citizens, who would presumably respond likewise or face the guillotine. The beginning of revolutions is psychologically strikingly akin to that of certain relationships – the stress on unity, the belief in the omnipotence of the couple/nation, the urge to give up on previous egotism, to dissolve the boundaries of the self, the desire that there be no more secrets [the fear of the opposite soon leading to lover's paranoia and/or the creation of a secret police].

15.   But if the beginnings of love and amorous politics are equally rosy, then the ends may be equally bloody. Are we not already familiar with the phenomenon of love that ends in tyranny, where the rulers' firm conviction that they have the true interests of the nation at heart ends by justifying the right to kill all those who disagree with the faith? In so far as love is a faith [and it is many things beside], it is illiberal, for no faith has ever been free of an inclination to vent its frustration on

dissenters and heretics. Put another way, as soon as one has a faith in something [*la patrie*, Marxism-Leninism, National Socialism], the strength of that faith must automatically banish alternatives.

16.   A few days after the shoe incident, I went to the newsagent to pick up a paper and a carton of milk. Mr Paul told me he'd just run out of the milk, but that if I could wait a moment, he'd get another crate in from the storeroom. Watching him walk out towards the back of the shop, I noticed Mr Paul was wearing a pair of thick grey socks and brown leather sandals. They were spectacularly ugly, but curiously enough, spectacularly inoffensive. Why could I not remain similarly composed in the face of Chloe's shoes? Why could I not enjoy the same cordiality with the woman I loved as with the newsagent who sold me my daily bread?

17.   The wish to replace the butcher-butchered relationship with a newsagent one has long dominated political thinking. Why could rulers not act politely towards their citizens, tolerating sandals, dissent and divergence? The answer from liberal thinkers is that cordiality can arise only once rulers give up talk of governing for the *love* of their citizens, and concentrate instead on getting interest rates down and the trains running on time.

18.   Safe politics finds its greatest apologist in John Stuart Mill, who in 1859 published the classic defence of loveless liberalism, *On Liberty*, a ringing plea that citizens should simply be left alone by the state [however well-meaning it was] and not

be told to change their shoes or read certain books or clean their ears or floss their teeth. Mill argued that though an ancient commonwealth [not to mention Robespierre's France] had felt itself entitled to hold 'a deep interest in the whole bodily and mental discipline of every one of its citizens', the modern state should as much as possible stand back and leave its citizens alone. Like a harassed partner in a relationship who begs simply to be given space, Mill asked that the state leave citizens to themselves:

> The only freedom which deserves the name is that of pursuing our own good, in our own way, so long as we do not attempt to deprive others of theirs, or impede their efforts to obtain it . . . The only purpose for which power can be rightfully exercised over any member of a civilized society against his will is to prevent harm to others. His own good, either physical or moral, is not sufficient warrant.[2]

19.   Mill's pleas sound so rational, could one not apply such tenets to the personal sphere? Applied to a relationship, though, his vision seems sadly to lose much of its appeal. It evokes certain rather crusty marriages, where love has evaporated long ago, and where the couple sleeps in separate bedrooms, exchanging the occasional word when they meet in the kitchen before work, a relationship where both partners have long ago given up hope of mutual understanding, settling instead for a tepid friendship based on controlled misunderstanding, polite-

[2] *On Liberty*, John Stuart Mill, Cambridge University Press, 1989

ness while they get through the evening's shepherd's pie, 3 a.m. bitterness at the emotional failure that surrounds them.

20.   We are back to the choice between love and liberalism, a *choice* because the latter only seems truly practical in a distant relationship or once indifference has set in. The sandals of the newsagent did not annoy me because I did not care about the newsagent, I wished to get my paper and milk from him, but no more. I did not wish to bare my soul or cry on his shoulder, so his footwear remained unobtrusive. But had I fallen in love with Mr Paul, could I really have continued to face his sandals with such equanimity, or would there not have come a point when [out of love] I would have cleared my throat and suggested an alternative?

21.   If my relationship with Chloe never reached the levels of the Terror, it was perhaps because we were able to temper the choice between love and liberalism with an ingredient that too few relationships and even fewer amorous politicians [Lenin, Pol Pot, Robespierre] have ever possessed, an ingredient that might just [were there enough of it to go around] save both states and couples from intolerance; namely a sense of humour.

22.   It seems significant that revolutionaries share with lovers a tendency towards great earnestness. It is as hard to imagine cracking a joke with Stalin as with Young Werther – both of them seem desperately, though differently, intense. And with the inability to laugh comes an inability to acknowledge the relativity of things human, the contradictions inherent in a society or relationship, the multiplicity and clash of desires, the

need to accept that one's partner will never learn how to park a car, or wash out a bath or give up a taste for Joni Mitchell – but that one loves them nevertheless.

23. If Chloe and I were able to transcend certain of our differences, it was because we had the will to make jokes of the impasses we found in one another's characters. I could not stop hating Chloe's shoes, she continued to like them, I loved her, but [after the window was patched] we at least found room to turn the incident into a joke. By threatening to 'defenestrate' oneself whenever arguments became heated, one was always able to draw a laugh from the other, and hence help neutralize a frustration. My driving techniques could not be improved, but they earned me the name 'Alain Prost', Chloe's occasional martyr-trips I found wearing, but less so when I could obey her as 'Joan of Arc'. Humour meant there was no need for a direct confrontation, one could glide over an irritant, winking at it obliquely, making a criticism without actually needing to *speak it* ['By this joke I let you know that I hate *x* without needing to tell you so – your laughter acknowledges the criticism'].

24. It is a sign that two people have stopped loving one another [or at least stopped wishing to make the effort that constitutes ninety per cent of love] when they are no longer able to spin differences into jokes. Humour lined the walls of irritation between our ideals and the reality: behind each joke, there was a warning of difference, of disappointment even, but it was a difference that had been defused – and could therefore be passed over without the need for a pogrom.

CHAPTER NINE

BEAUTY

1.   Does beauty give birth to love or does love give birth to beauty? Did I love Chloe because she was beautiful or was she beautiful because I loved her? Surrounded by an infinite number of people, we may ask [staring at our lover while they talk on the phone or lie opposite us in the bath] why our desire has chosen to settle on this particular face, this particular mouth or nose or ear, why this curve of the neck or dimple in the cheek has come to answer so precisely to our criteria of perfection? Every one of our lovers offers different solutions to the problem of beauty, and yet succeeds in redefining our amorous aesthetics in a way that is as original and as idiosyncratic as the landscape of their face.

2.   If Marsilio Ficino [1433–99] defined love as 'the desire for beauty', in what ways did Chloe fulfil this desire? To listen to Chloe, in no way whatsoever. No amount of reassuring could persuade her that she was anything but monstrously ugly. She insisted on finding her nose too small, her mouth too wide, her chin uninteresting, her ears too round, her eyes not green enough, her hair not wavy enough, her breasts too small, her feet too large, her hands too wide, and her wrists too narrow. She would gaze longingly at the faces in the pages of *Elle* and

Vogue and declare that the concept of a just God was – in the light of her physical appearance – simply an incoherence.

3.   Chloe believed that beauty could be measured according to an objective standard, one she had quite simply failed to reach. Without acknowledging it as such, Chloe was resolutely attached to a Platonic concept of beauty, an aesthetic she shared with the editors of the world's fashion magazines and that would fuel a sense of daily self-loathing in front of the mirror. According to Plato and the editor of *Vogue*, there exists such a thing as an ideal Form of beauty, made up of a balanced relation between parts, which earthly bodies will resemble to a greater or a lesser degree. Everything we consider beautiful, said Plato, partakes in the essential Form of beauty, and must hence exhibit universal characteristics. Take a beautiful woman and you will see there is a mathematical basis for this beauty, an inherent balance that is no less precise than that found in the construction of a classical temple. The face on the front cover of a magazine is, Plato would have suggested, one of the closer human approximations of the ideal of beauty [and Chloe worshipped it for just that reason. I have an image of her sitting on the bed drying her hair and flicking through the pages, twisting her face to caricature the effortless pose of the models portrayed]. Chloe was ashamed that her nose did not match the dimensions of her lips. Her nose was small, and her lips were large, which meant that there must have been a Platonic disharmony in the centre of her face. Plato had said that only when elements match is there the proper balance that gives an object a dynamic stillness and self-completeness, and that is just what must have been lacking. If Plato had said that only 'the qualities of measure

(*metron*) and proportion (*symmetron*) invariably constitute beauty and excellence', then Chloe's face must have been lacking in both beauty and excellence.

4. Whatever the disharmonies in her face, Chloe found the rest of her body even more unbalanced. Whereas I loved to watch the soap running over her stomach and down her legs when we showered together, whenever she looked at herself in the mirror, she would invariably declare that something was 'lopsided' – though quite what was lopsided I never discovered. Leon Battista Alberti [1409–72] might have known better, for he believed that a beautiful body had certain fixed proportions sculptors should know about and that could be discovered by dividing the body into six hundred units, for which he worked out an ideal distance of part to part. In his book *On Scuplture*, Alberti defined beauty as 'a Harmony of all the Parts, in whatsoever Subject it appears, fitted together with such proportion and connection, that nothing could be added, diminished or altered, but for the worse'. According to Chloe however, almost anything about her body could have been added, diminished or altered without for that matter spoiling anything that nature had not already ruined.

5. But clearly Plato and Leon Battista Alberti [however sound their calculations] must have neglected to include something in their aesthetic theory, for I found Chloe devastatingly beautiful. I hesitate to describe what exactly it was that I found so attractive. Did I like her green eyes, her dark hair, her full mouth? I hesitate in answering, because of the difficulty of ever explaining in words why one person is attractive and another is

not. I could talk of the freckles on her nose or the curve of her neck, but what would it do to convince someone who did not find her attractive? Beauty is after all not something that one can ever *convince* someone else about. It is not like a mathematical formula, through which one may lead someone and arrive at an incontestable conclusion. Debates over the attractiveness of men and women are like the debates between art historians, attempting to justify why one painting is superior to another. A Van Gogh or a Gauguin? The only way to make a case for one or the other would be by an attempted redescription of the work in language ['the lyrical intelligence of Gauguin's South Sea skies . . .' next to 'the Wagnerian depth of Van Gogh's blues . . .'] or else by an elucidation of technique or materials ['the Expressionist feel of Van Gogh's later years . . .' 'Gauguin's Cezanne-like linearity . . .']. But what would all this be doing to actually explain why one painting *works*, affects us, grips us by the collar with its beauty? And if painters have traditionally disdained art historians who come in their wake, it is perhaps not so much out of inverted snobbery as out of a sense that the language of paint [the language of beauty] cannot be collapsed into the language of words.

6.   It was not *beauty* that I could hence hope to describe, only my own subjective response to Chloe's appearance. I could not claim to be laying down an aesthetic theory of universal validity, I could simply point out where my desire had happened to settle, while allowing the possibility that others would not locate the same perfections in the same body. In so doing, I was forced to reject the Platonic idea of an objective criterion of beauty, siding instead with Kant's view [expressed in his

Critique of Judgement] that aesthetic judgements were ones 'whose determining ground can be no other than subjective'.

7.   The Kantian view of aesthetics holds that the proportions of a body are ultimately not as important as the subjective way in which that body is viewed. How else can we explain why the same body may be considered beautiful by one person and ugly by another? The phenomenon of beauty residing in the eye of the beholder can be compared to the famous Müller–Lyer illusion [see fig 9.1], where two lines of identical length will appear to be of different size because of the different arrows attached on the end. If length can be likened to beauty, the way that I gazed at Chloe functioned like the arrows on the end of the two lines, it is what marked out Chloe's face as different, more beautiful [longer] than one which might objectively have been almost the same. My love was like the arrows that had been placed on the ends of identical lines but that gave an impression, however fictitious, of difference.

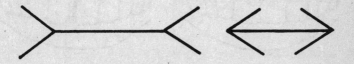

Figure 9.1   Müller–Lyer illusion

8.   Stendhal famously defined beauty as 'the promise of happiness', a definition far from the rigidity of the Platonic idea of perfect harmony of part to part. Chloe may not have been

endowed with classical perfection, but she was beautiful nevertheless. Did she make me happy because she was beautiful, or was she beautiful because she made me happy? It was a self-confirming circle: I found Chloe beautiful when she made me happy, and she made me happy by being beautiful.

9.   Yet what was distinctive about my attraction was that it was based not on the obvious targets of desire, as much as on precisely those features that might have been considered imperfect by someone considering Chloe from a Platonic perspective. There was a certain pride in locating desire in the awkward features of her face, in precisely those areas where others would not look. I did not for instance see the gap in between her two front teeth [see fig 9.2] as an offensive deviation from an ideal arrangement, but as an original and most love-worthy redefinition of dental perfection. I was not simply indifferent to the gap in between the teeth, I positively adored it.

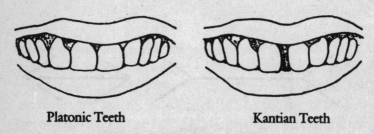

Platonic Teeth   Kantian Teeth

Figure 9.2

10.   I adored the secrecy, the difficulty of my desire, the fact that no one could have guessed the meaning of Chloe's teeth

for me. She would not have been considered beautiful in the eyes of a Platonist, in certain lights she might even have been considered ugly, but then her beauty had something that a platonically perfect face lacked. Beauty was to be found in the area of oscillation between ugliness and classical perfection. A face that launches a thousand ships is not always architecturally formal: it can be as unstable as an object that is spinning between two colours and that gives rise to a third shade so long as it is moving. There is a certain tyranny about perfection, a certain exhaustion about it even, something that denies the viewer a role in its creation and that asserts itself with all the dogmatism of an unambiguous statement. True beauty cannot be measured because it is fluctuating, it has only a few angles from which it may be seen, and then not in all lights and at all times. It flirts dangerously with ugliness, it takes risks with itself, it does not side comfortably with mathematical rules of proportion, it draws its appeal from precisely those areas that will also lend themselves to ugliness. Beauty may need to take a calculated risk with ugliness.

11.   Proust once said that classically beautiful women should be left to men without imagination, and it is perhaps because of its attractions to my imagination that the gap in Chloe's teeth proved so seductive. The imagination enjoyed playing in the little space, closing it, reopening it, calling for my tongue to run down it. The gap allowed me to play a role in the arrangement of Chloe's dental features, her beauty was fractured enough that it could support certain creative rearrangements. Because her face had evidence within it for both beauty and ugliness, my imagination was given a role in holding on to the precarious

thread of beauty. In its ambiguity, Chloe's face could be compared to Wittgenstein's duck-rabbit [see fig 9.3], where both a duck and a rabbit seem contained in the same image, much as there seemed to be two faces contained within Chloe's features.

Figure 9.3   Wittgenstein's Duck-Rabbit

12.   In Wittgenstein's example, much depends on the attitude of the viewer: if the imagination is looking for a duck, it will find one, if it is looking for a rabbit, then it too will appear. There is evidence for both, so what counts is the predisposition, the mental set, of the viewer. What was of course providing me with a beautiful image of Chloe [rather than a duck] was love. I felt that this love must have been more genuine because it had not settled on a face that was obviously, unambiguously proportioned. The editor of *Vogue* might have had difficulty including photos of Chloe in an issue, but ironically, this only reinforced my desire, for it seemed a confirmation of the uniqueness that I had managed to find in her. How original is it to find a classically proportioned person 'beautiful'? It surely takes greater effort, greater Proustian imagination, to locate beauty in a gap

between the teeth. In finding Chloe beautiful, I had not settled on the obvious, I could perhaps see in her features things that others could not see: I had animated her face with her soul.

13. The danger with the kind of beauty that does not look like a Greek statue is that its precariousness places much emphasis on the viewer. Once the imagination decides to remove itself from the gap in the teeth, is it not time for a good orthodontist? Once we locate beauty in the eye of the beholder, what will happen when the beholder looks elsewhere? But perhaps that was all part of Chloe's appeal. A subjective theory of beauty makes the observer wonderfully indispensable.

CHAPTER TEN

SPEAKING LOVE

1.   In the middle of May, Chloe celebrated her twenty-fourth birthday. She had long been dropping hints in relation to a red pullover in the window of a shop in Piccadilly, so the evening before, I stopped off on my way back from work and bought it for her, wrapped in blue paper with a pink bow. But in the course of preparing a card to accompany the package, I suddenly came to realize, my pen hovering over the paper, that I had never told Chloe I loved her.

2.   A declaration would perhaps not have been unexpected [particularly when accompanied by a red pullover], yet the fact it had never been made was significant. Pullovers may be a sign of love between a man and a woman, but we had yet to translate them into a language beyond knitwear. It was as though the core of our relationship, configured around the word *love*, was somehow unmentionable, either not worthy of mention, or too significant to have yet had time for formulation.

3.   It was easier to understand why Chloe had not said anything. She was suspicious of words. '*One can talk problems into existence,*' she had once said, and just as problems could be fashioned out of language, so love could be destroyed by it. I

remembered a story she had told me. At the age of twelve, her parents had sent her on a camping holiday organized by a youth group. There she had fallen madly in love with a boy her age, and after much blushing and hesitation, they had ended up taking a walk around the lake together. By a shaded bank, the boy asked her to sit down, and after a moment, took her damp hand in his. It was the first time a boy had held her hand. She felt so elated, she had to tell him [with all the earnestness of a twelve-year-old] that he was 'the best thing that had ever happened to her'. But she should not have spoken. The next day, she discovered her words had spread all over camp, her foolishly honest declaration replayed in a mockery of her vulnerability. She had experienced a betrayal at the hands of language, the way intimate words may be converted to a common currency, and therefore had come to trust the body instead, the movement rather than the phrase.

4.   With her customary resistance to the rose-tinted, Chloe would probably have shrugged a declaration off with a joke, not because she did not want to hear, but because any formulation would have seemed dangerously close to both complete cliché and total nakedness. It was not that Chloe was unsentimental, she was simply too discreet with her emotions to speak them in the worn, social language of the *romantic* [love mediated]. Though her feelings may have been directed towards me, in a curious sense, *they were not for me to know*.

5.   Yet my pen was still hesitating over her birthday card [a picture of a giraffe blowing out candles on the cover], and I felt that whatever her resistance, the occasion of her birthday [full

of the absurd reverence accorded to one's genesis] called for a linguistic confirmation of the bond between us. I tried to imagine what she would make of the parcel I would hand her, not the red pullover, but the parcel of words that spoke of love. I tried to imagine her alone, in the Underground on the way to work, or in the bath or street, opening it at her own pace, attempting to make out for herself what the man who loved her had meant by giving her such curious objects.

6.   The difficulty of a declaration goes beyond the difficulty of ordinary communication. If I had told Chloe I had a stomach ache or a red car or a garden full of daffodils, I could count on her to understand. Naturally, my image of a be-daffodiled garden might slightly differ from hers, but there would be reasonable parity between the two images. The words, crossing the divide that separated us, would have operated as reliable messengers of meaning, the letter would have reached its destination. But the card I was now trying to write had no such guarantee attached to it. The words were the most ambiguous in the language, because the thing they referred to so sorely lacked stable meaning. Certainly, travellers had returned from the heart and tried to represent what they had seen, but the word was on no fixed latitude, it lacked geographical definition, it was a rare coloured butterfly never conclusively identified.

7.   The thought was a lonely one: of the error one may find over a single word, an argument not for pedants, but of desperate importance to lovers who are sick of talking through interpreters. We could both speak of being in love, and yet this love might mean wholly different things within each of us.

Sending out words of love was like firing a coded message with a faulty transmitter, always unsure of how it would be received [yet one nevertheless had to send, like the dandelion releasing numberless spores of which only a fraction would reproduce, a random, optimistic telecommunication effort – trust in the postal service].

8.   Language was all I had to bridge the divide. Would she understand the meaning I had tried to fill this leaky sieve with? How much of my love would be left by the time it reached her? We could have a dialogue in a language that seemed in common, only then to discover that the words had roots in different sources. Often we had read the same books at night in the same bed, and later realized they had touched us in different places, had been different books for each of us. Might the same divergence therefore not occur over a single love-line?

My heart > > > – l – o — v — e —— > *Her heart*
LANGUAGE

Figure 10.1

9.   But nor were the words wholly in my hands. They had been in too many others' before mine, I had been born *into* language [though this was not my birthday], I had not invented the disease myself – and with this second-handedness came both problems and advantages. Advantages because there was a common area that had over centuries been parcelled off as belonging to love. Though we might not agree over what we felt towards one another, Chloe and I were good enough

105

students to know love was not hate and to recognize the region Hollywood stars travelled in when they downed their martinis and spoke its name.

10.   Our perceptions of love were soaked in the social tub of the romantic. When I daydreamed of Chloe, those dreams necessarily merged with elements of the soft, caramel vision of a hundred and one media embraces. I was not just in love with Chloe, I was at the same time participating in a social ritual. When I listened in the car to the lyrics of the latest pop songs, did not my love blend effortlessly with the soaring voice of the artist, was it not Chloe that I found in the eloquent lyrics of another?

> *Wouldn't it be nice*
> *To hold you in my arms*
> *And love you, baby?*
> *To hold you in my arms*
> *Oh yeah, and love you baby?*

11.   Love is not self-explanatory, it is always *interpreted* by the culture in which we celebrate our birthday. How did I know that what I felt for Chloe was *love* without others to prompt me to an answer? That I identified with the singer on the car radio did not imply a spontaneous understanding of the phenomenon. If I believed myself to be in love, was this not simply the result of living in a particular cultural epoch that sought out and worshipped the drooling heart wherever it could? Was it not society, rather than any pre-communal urges on my part, that had been the motivating factor? In previous cultures and ages,

would I not have been taught to ignore the feelings I had for Chloe [in the way I was now taught to ignore the impulse to wear stockings or respond to insult with a challenge to a duel]?

12. *'Some people would never have fallen in love if they had never heard of love,'* aphorized La Rochefoucauld, and does not history prove him right? I was due to take Chloe to a Chinese restaurant in Camden, but declarations of love might have seemed more appropriate elsewhere given the scant regard traditionally given to love in Chinese culture. According to the psychological anthropologist L. K. Hsu, whereas Western cultures are 'individual-centred' and place great emphasis on emotions, in contrast, Chinese culture is 'situation-centred' and concentrates on groups rather than couples and their love [though the manager of the Lao Tzu was nevertheless delighted to take my booking]. Love is never a given, it is constructed and defined by different societies. In at least one society, the Manu of New Guinea, there is not even a word for love. In other cultures, love exists, but is given particular forms. Ancient Egyptian love poetry has no interest in the emotions of shame, guilt or ambivalence. The Greeks thought nothing of homosexuality, Christianity proscribed the body and eroticized the soul, the Troubadours equated lover with unrequited passion, the Romantics made love into a religion, and the happily married S. M. Greenfield, in an article in the *Sociological Quarterly* [6, 361–377] writes that love is today kept alive by modern capitalism only in order to:

'. . . motivate individuals – where there is no other means of motivating them – to occupy the positions husband-father and wife-mother and form nuclear families that are essential not only for reproduction and socialization but also to maintain the existing arrangements for distributing and consuming goods and services and, in general, to keep the social system in proper working order and thus maintaining it as a going concern.'

13. Anthropology and history are full of divergences [and hence horrors for those standing somewhere in time] when it comes to sexuality. In mid-Victorian Britain, a woman who masturbated could be considered insane and locked up in an asylum for doing so. In New Guinea, there was a belief that 'manhood' was embodied in male semen, and there was a custom of ritual semen eating among young males. In the New Guinean village of Iwi, there was even at one time a custom of eating the penises of men who had been killed in order to gain strength. Mangaian girls had their clitorises stretched, while in Maasai society, a girl who reached puberty had her clitoris and labia minora excised, which was said to remove 'the dirt of childhood'. Gender crossing existed among American Indians and men captured in war were in some tribes taken into the victor's home with the status of a wife.

14. Society, like a good stationery shop, had equipped me with a set of labels to affix to the flutters of the heart. The sickness, nausea and longing I had at times felt at the thought of Chloe, my society filed under 'L', but across oceans or centuries, the filing cabinet might have had another index. Could my symptoms not easily have been identified as signs of

a religious visitation, a viral infection or even a non-metaphoric coronary attack? When St Teresa of Avila [1515–82], founder of the Discalced Carmelite Order, spoke of something psycho-detectives might today call a sublimated orgasm, she described experiencing the love of God through the visit of an angel, a boy who was

'. . . very beautiful, his face so aflame that he appeared to be one of the highest types of angels who seem to be all afire . . . In his hands I saw a golden spear and at the end of the iron tip I seemed to see a point of fire. With this he seemed to pierce my heart several times so that it pen-etrated my entrails . . . The pain was so sharp that it made me utter several moans; and so excessive was the sweetness caused me by this intense pain that one can never wish to lose it, nor will one's soul be content with anything less than God.'

15.   In the end, I decided that a card with a giraffe was not the best place to speak of love, and that I would wait till dinner. I drove to Chloe's apartment at eight o'clock in order to pick her up and give her the present. She was delighted that I had taken up her hints over the Piccadilly window, the only regret [tactfully delivered a few days later] was that it had been the blue and not the red one she'd been pointing to [though receipts gave us a second chance].

16.   The restaurant could not have been more romantic. All around us in the Lao Tzu, couples much like ourselves [though our subjective sense of uniqueness did not allow us to think so]

were holding hands, drinking wine and fumbling with chop-sticks.

'God, I feel better, I must have been starving. I've been so depressed all day,' said Chloe.

'Why?'

'Because I have this thing about birthdays, they always remind me of death and forced jollity. But actually, I think this one's turning out to be not so bad in the end. In fact, it's pretty all right, thanks to a little help from my friend.'

She looked up at me and smiled.

'You know where I was this time last year?' she asked.

'No, where?'

'Being taken out for dinner by my horrible aunt. It was awful, I kept having to go to the bathroom to cry, I was so upset that it was my birthday and the only person who'd invited me out was my aunt with this irritating stutter who couldn't stop telling me she didn't understand how a nice girl like me didn't have a man in her life. So it's probably no bad thing I ran into you . . .'

17. She really was adorable [thought the lover, at the pinnacle of subjective judgement]. But how could I tell her so in a way that would suggest the distinctive nature of my attraction? Words like *love* or *devotion* or *infatuation* were exhausted by the weight of successive love stories, by the layers imposed on them through the uses of others. At the moment when I most wanted language to be original, personal and completely private, I came up against the irrevocably public nature of the language of the heart.

18.   The restaurant was of no help, for its romantic setting made love too conspicuous, hence insincere. The romantic weakened the bond between authorial intent and language, the signifieds kept threatening infidelity [particularly when a recording of Chopin's *Nocturnes* played over the loudspeakers and a candle had been set between us on the table]. There seemed to be no way to transport *love* in the word L-O-V-E, without at the same time throwing the most banal associations into the basket. There needed to be an identification with L-O-V-E, but however hard I tried the word was too rich in foreign history: everything from the Troubadours to *Casablanca* had cashed in on those letters.

19.   There is always the option of being emotionally lazy, that is, of *quoting*. I could reach for the public *Dictionary of Received Love*, with its ready-made pouches to fit the mood, sticky with lies and caramel. Yet there was something repugnant in the idea, like sleeping in another's dirty sheets. Was it not a duty to be the author of my own romantic dialogue? Would I not have to fashion a declaration to match Chloe's uniqueness?

20.   It is always easier to quote others than to speak for oneself, easier to use Shakespeare or Sinatra than risk one's own sore throat. Born into language, we necessarily adopt the use others have made of it, involving ourselves in a history that is not our own. For lovers who feel they are reinventing the world through their love, there is an inevitable confrontation with a history that preceded their union [be it their own past or that of society]. My every loving gesture had a birthday that predated

111

Chloe – there were always other birthdays, there could be no virginal declarations [even twelve-year-old Chloe by the lake was already involved, if only by virtue of a television]. Like making love, speaking of it involved me with a trace of everyone I had ever slept with.

21.   There were therefore slivers of others in everything. In my food and in my thoughts, there was alterity. When I wished there to be only Chloe, there was an incestuous involvement with culture: *a man and a woman, lovers, celebrating a birthday in a Chinese restaurant, one night in the Western world, somewhere towards the end of the twentieth century*. I felt a disconcerting rub with the mundanity of my striking originality – in holding Chloe's hand, in thinking I loved her. I now understood Chloe's hatred of birthdays, our arbitrary insertion on the conveyor belt of culture. My desire impelled me to leave the linear and search for metaphor. My meaning would never make the journey in L-O-V-E. It would have to seek alternative transportation, perhaps in a boat that was somewhat deformed, that was stretched or shrunk, or was invisible – not representing *the thing*, so as better to capture its mystery, love as Hebrew God.

22.   Then I noticed a small plate of complimentary marshmallows near Chloe's elbow. Inexplicably from a semantic point of view, it suddenly seemed clear to me that I did not *love* Chloe so much as *marshmallow* her. What it was about a marshmallow that should suddenly have accorded so perfectly with my feelings towards her, I will never know, but the word seemed to capture the essence of my amorous state with an accuracy that the word love, weary with over-use, simply could not aspire to. Even

more inexplicably, when I took Chloe's hand and, with a wink at Bogart and Romeo, told her that I had something very important to tell her, that I *marshmallowed* her, she seemed to understand perfectly, answering it was the sweetest thing anyone had ever told her.

23.   And from then on, love was, for Chloe and me at least, no longer simply *love*, it was a sugary, puffy object a few millimetres in diameter that melts deliciously in the mouth.

CHAPTER ELEVEN

WHAT DO YOU SEE
IN HER?

1.   Summer flew in with the first week of June, making a Mediterranean city of London, drawing people from their homes and offices into the parks and squares. The heat coincided with the arrival of a new colleague at work, an American architect, who had been hired to spend six months working with us on an office complex near Waterloo.

2.   'They told me it rained every day in London – and look at this!' remarked Will as we sat one lunchtime in a restaurant in Covent Garden. 'Incredible, and I brought only pullovers.'
     'Don't worry Will, they have T-shirts here too.'
     I had first met William Knott five years ago, when we had spent a term together at the Rhode Island School of Design. He was an immensely tall man, with the perpetual tan, intrepid smile and rugged face of an explorer. Since finishing his studies at Berkley, he had developed a successful career on the West Coast, where he was considered one of the most innovative and intelligent architects of his generation.

3.   'So tell me, are you seeing anyone?' asked Will as we began our coffee. 'You're not still with what's her name, that . . .?'

'No, no, that finished long ago. I'm involved in something serious now.'

'Great, tell me about it.'

'Well, you must come over for dinner and meet her.'

'I'd love to. Tell me more.'

'She's called Chloe, she's twenty-four, she's a graphic designer. She's intelligent, beautiful, very funny . . .'

'It sounds terrific.'

'How about you?'

'Nothing to say really, I was dating this girl from UCLA, but you know, we were getting in each other's head-space, so we sort of both pulled the rip-cord. We weren't ready to ride the big one together, so . . . But tell me more about this Chloe, what is it you see in her?'

4.   *What did I see in her?* The question came back to me later that evening in the middle of Safeway, watching Chloe at the till, enraptured by the way she went about packing the groceries into a plastic bag. The charm I detected in these trivial gestures revealed a readiness to accept almost anything as incontestable proof she was perfect. *What did I see in her?* Almost everything.

5.   For a moment, I fantasized I might transform myself into a carton of yogurt so as to undergo the same process of being gently and thoughtfully accommodated by her into a shopping bag between a tin of tuna and a bottle of olive oil. It was only the incongruously unsentimental atmosphere of the supermarket ['Liver Promotion Week'] that alerted me to how far I might have been sliding into romantic pathology.

6.   On the way back to the car, I complimented Chloe on the adorable way she had gone about the business of doing the grocery shopping.

'Don't be so silly,' she replied. 'Can you open the boot, the keys are in my bag.'

7.   To detect charm in out of the way places is to refuse to be bewitched by the obvious. It is easy enough to find charm in a pair of eyes or the contours of a well-shaped mouth. How much harder to detect it in the movements of a woman's hand across a supermarket check-out. Chloe's mannerisms were the signs of a wider perfection a lover could find. They were like the tips of an iceberg, an indication of what lay beneath. Did it not require a lover to discern their true value, a value that would naturally seem meaningless to someone less curious, less in love?

8.   Yet I remained pensive on the drive home through the evening rush hour. My love began to question itself. What did it mean if things I considered charming about Chloe, she considered incidental or irrelevant to her true self. Was I reading things into Chloe that simply did not belong to her? I looked at the slope of her shoulders and the way that a strand of her hair was trapped in the car head-rest. She turned towards me and smiled, so for an instant I saw the gap in between her two front teeth. How much of my sensitive, soulful lover lay in my fellow passenger?

9.   Love reveals its insanity by its refusal to acknowledge the inherent *normality* of the loved one. Hence the boredom of lovers for those standing on the side-lines. What do they see in

the beloved save simply another human being? I had often tried to share my enthusiasm for Chloe with friends, with whom in the past I had found much common ground over films, books and politics, but who now looked at me with the secular puzzlement of atheists faced with messianic fervour. After the tenth time of telling friends these stories of Chloe at the dry cleaner or Chloe and me at the cinema, or Chloe and I buying a take-away, these stories with no plot and less action, just the central character standing in the centre of an almost motionless tale, I was forced to acknowledge that love was a lonely pursuit, one that could at best be understood by one other person, the loved one themselves.

10.   Only a thin line separates love from fantasy, from a belief holding no connection with outer reality, an essentially private, narcissistic obsession. There was of course nothing inherently lovable about Chloe's way·of packing the groceries, love was merely something I had decided to ascribe to her gesture, a gesture that might have been interpreted very differently by others in line with us at Safeway. A person is never good or bad *per se*, which means that loving or hating them necessarily has at its basis a subjective, and perhaps illusionistic element. I was reminded of the way Will's question had made the distinction between qualities that belonged to a person and those ascribed to them by their lover. For Will had not asked me *who* Chloe was [how could a lover be so objective?], but rather what I *saw* in her – a far more subjective and perhaps unreliable perception.

11.   Shortly after her older brother died, Chloe [who had just celebrated her eighth birthday] went through a deeply philos-

ophical stage. 'I began to question everything,' she told me, 'I had to figure out what death was, that's enough to turn anyone into a philosopher.' One of her great obsessions, to which allusions were still made in her family, concerned thoughts familiar to readers of Descartes and Berkeley. Chloe would put her hand over her eyes and tell the family her brother was still alive because she could see him in her mind just as she could see them. Why did they tell her he was dead if she could see him in her own mind? Then, in a further challenge to reality and because of the way she felt towards them, Chloe would [with the grin of a six-year-old child facing the power of its hostile impulses] tell her parents she could kill them by shutting her eyes and never thinking of them again – a plan that no doubt elicited a predictably unphilosophical response.

12.   Love and death seem naturally to invite questions of inner wish and outer reality, the former leading us to draw a belief in its outer existence, the latter in its absence. Whatever and whoever Chloe was, could I not shut my eyes and believe my perception to be reality, that what I saw in her really was there, whatever she or the crowd at Safeway thought?

13.   Yet solipsism had its limits. Were my views of Chloe anywhere near reality, or had I completely lost judgement? Certainly she *seemed* lovable to me, but was she *actually* as lovable as I thought? It was the old Cartesian colour problem: the bus might *seem* red to a viewer, but was this bus actually red in and of its essence? When Will met Chloe a few weeks later, he certainly had his doubts, unexpressed of course, but written all over his behaviour and in the way he told me at work the

next day that for a Californian, English women were of course 'very special'.

14.   To be honest, Chloe gave me the occasional doubt herself. One night, I remember her sitting in my living-room reading while we listened to a Bach cantata I had set spinning on the record player. The music sang of heavenly fires, Lord's blessings and beloved companions, while Choe's face, tired, but happy, bathed by a streak of light crossing the darkened room from the desk lamp, seemed as though it belonged to an angel, an angel who was only elaborately pretending [with trips to Safeway or the Post Office] that she was an ordinary mortal, but whose mind was in fact filled with the most delicate, subtle and divine thoughts.

15.   Because only the body is open to the eye, the hope of the infatuated lover is the soul's fidelity to its casing, the hope that the body owns an appropriate soul, that what the skin *represents* turns out to be what it *is*. I did not love Chloe *for* her body, I loved her body for the promise of who she was. It was a most inspiring promise.

16.   Yet what if her face were a *trompe-l'oeil*, a mask, a surface suggesting an interior it did not possess? To return to Will's implicit distinction, what if I was only seeing things in/-to her? I knew there were faces that suggested qualities they did not have, there were children whose eyes were filled with a wisdom they were too young to have earned. '*By forty, everyone has the face they deserve*,' wrote George Orwell, but is that ever true, or is it not simply a myth as comforting in the world of facial

appearance as it is in the economic sphere, namely the belief in a form of natural justice? To recognize the myth would be to confront the awful facial lottery of nature, hence to give up our belief in a God-given [or at least *meaningfully* given] face.

17.   The lover, standing back at the supermarket counter or in the living-room, watches the beloved and begins to dream, to interpret their face and their gestures, locating in them something other-worldly, perfect, enchanted. He or she takes the way the beloved packs a tin of tuna fish or pours the tea to form the ingredients of a dream. Yet does not life always force them to be light sleepers, always liable to be awoken to more mundane realities?

18.   'Can't you turn off this impossible yodelling,' said the angel all of a sudden.

'What impossible yodelling?'

'You know, the music.'

'It's Bach.'

'I know, but it sounds so silly, I can't concentrate on *Cosmo*.'

19.   Is it really *her* I love, I thought to myself as I looked again at Chloe reading on the sofa across the room, or simply an idea that collects itself around her mouth, her eyes, her face? In extending her expression to her whole character, was I not perhaps guilty of mistaken metonymy, the metonym as symbol, an attribute of an entity substituted for the entity itself? The crown for the monarchy, the wheel for the car, the White House

for the US government, Chloe's angelic expression for Chloe . . .

20.   In the oasis complex, the thirsty man imagines he sees water, palm trees and shade not because he has evidence for the belief, but because he has a need for it. Desperate needs bring about a hallucination of their solution: thirst hallucinates water, the need for love hallucinates the ideal man or woman. The oasis complex is never a complete delusion: the man in the desert does see *something* on the horizon. It is just that the palms have withered, the well is dry and the place infected with locusts.

21.   Was I not victim of a similar delusion, alone in a room with a woman who wore the face of someone composing *The Divine Comedy* while working her way through the *Cosmopolitan* astrology section?

CHAPTER TWELVE

SCEPTICISM AND FAITH

1.   By contrast with the history of love, the history of philosophy shows a relentless concern with the discrepancy between appearance and reality. 'I think I see a tree outside,' the philosopher mutters, 'but is it not possible that this is just an optical illusion behind my own retina?' 'I think I see my wife,' mutters the philosopher, adding hopefully, 'but is it not possible that she too is just an optical illusion?'

2.   Philosophers tend to limit epistemological doubt to the existence of tables, chairs, the courtyards of Cambridge colleges and the occasional unwanted wife. But to extend these questions to things that matter to us, to love for instance, is to raise the frightening possibility that the loved one is but an inner fantasy, with little connection to any objective reality.

3.   Doubt is easy when it is not a matter of survival: we are as sceptical as we can afford to be, and it is easiest to be sceptical about things that do not fundamentally sustain us. It is easy to doubt the existence of a table, it is hell to doubt the legitimacy of one's love.

4.   At the start of Western philosophical thinking, the progress from ignorance to knowledge finds itself likened by Plato

to a glorious journey from a dark cave into bright sunlight. Men are born unable to perceive reality, Plato tells us, much like cave dwellers who mistake shadows of objects thrown up on the walls for the objects themselves. Only with much effort may illusions be thrown off, and the journey made from the shadowy world of the cave into bright sunlight, where things can at last be seen for what they truly are. As with all allegories, this is a tale with a moral, the moral that the will to truth should constitute nothing less than the meaning of people's lives.

5.   It takes another twenty-three centuries or so until the Socratic assumption about the benefits of following this path from illusion to knowledge is challenged from a moral rather than a simply epistemological stand-point. Certainly everyone from Aristotle to Kant had criticized Plato on the *way* to reach the truth, but no one had seriously questioned the *value* of the undertaking. But in his *Beyond Good and Evil* [1886], Friedrich Nietzsche finally took the bull by the horns and asked.

> *What* in us really wants 'truth'? . . . We asked the *value* of this will. Suppose we want truth: *why not rather* untruth? and uncertainty? even ignorance? . . . The falseness of a judgement is to us not necessarily an objection to a judgement . . . the question is to what extent it is life-advancing, life-preserving, species-preserving, perhaps even species-breeding; and our fundamental tendency is to assert that the falsest judgements . . . are the most indispensable to us . . . that to renounce false judgements would be to renounce life, would be to deny life.[3]

[3] *Beyond Good and Evil*, Friedrich Nietzsche, Penguin, 1990

6.   From a religious point of view, the value of truth had of course been placed into question many centuries before. The philosopher Pascal [1623–62, hunchback Jansenist, *Pensées*] had talked of a choice facing every Christian in a world unevenly divided between the horror of a universe without God, and the blissful – but infinitely more remote – alternative that God did exist. Even though the odds were in favour of God not existing, Pascal argued that our faith could still be justified because the joys of the slimmer probability so far outweighed the horrors of the larger one. And so it should perhaps be with love. Lovers cannot remain philosophers for long, they should give way to the religious impulse, which is to believe and have faith, as opposed to the philosophic impulse, which is to doubt and enquire. They should prefer the risk of being *wrong and in love* to being *in doubt and without love*.

7.   Such thoughts were running through my mind one evening, sitting on Chloe's bed playing with her toy elephant Guppy. She'd told me that when she was a child, Guppy had played an enormous role in her life. He was a character as real as members of her family, and a lot more sympathetic. He had his own routines, his favourite foods, his own way of sleeping and talking – and yet, from a more dispassionate position, it was evident that Guppy was entirely her creation and had no existence outside her imagination. But if there was one thing that would have been ruinous to Chloe's relationship with the elephant, it would have been to ask her whether or not the creature really existed: *Does this furry thing actually live independently of you, or did you not simply invent him?* And it occurred to me then that perhaps a similar discretion should be applied to

124

lovers and their beloveds, that one should never ask a lover, *Does this love-stuffed person actually exist or are you simply imagining them?*

8.   Medical history tells us of the case of a man living under the peculiar delusion that he was a fried egg. Quite how or when this idea had entered his head, no one knew, but he now refused to sit down anywhere for fear that he would 'break himself' and 'spill the yolk'. His doctors tried sedatives and other drugs to appease his fears, but nothing seemed to work. Finally, one of them made the effort to enter the mind of the deluded patient and suggested he should carry a piece of toast with him at all times, which he could place on any chair he wished to sit on, and hence protect himself from spillage. From then on, the deluded man was never seen without a piece of toast handy, and was able to continue a more or less normal existence.

9.   What is the point of this story? It merely shows that though one may be living under a delusion [love, the belief that one is an egg], if one finds the complementary part of it [another lover like Chloe under a similar delusion, a piece of toast] then all may be well. Delusions are not harmful in themselves, they only hurt when one is alone in believing in them, when one cannot create an environment in which they can be sustained. So long as both Chloe and I could maintain a belief in the infinitely precarious soap bubble that is love, what did it matter whether or not the bus was really red?

CHAPTER THIRTEEN

INTIMACY

1.   Watching a cube of sugar dissolve into a cup of camomile tea, Chloe, whose company I relied upon to make life meaningful, remarked, 'We can't move in together because of my problem: I have to live on my own or else I melt. It's not just a question of shutting a door, it's a psychological, womb thing. It's not that I don't want you, it's that I'm afraid of wanting only you, of finding there's nothing left of me. So excuse it as part of my general fucked-upness, but I'm afraid I have to stay a bag lady.'

2.   I had first seen Chloe's bag at Heathrow airport, a bright pink cylinder with a luminous green shoulder strap. She had arrived at my door with it the first night she came to stay, once more apologizing for its offensive colours, saying she had used it to pack a toothbrush and a set of fresh clothes for the next day. I had assumed the bag would be a temporary feature, something to use before she would be comfortable enough to make clothes and a toothbrush resident in my flat. But she never gave up the bag, every morning she would repack it as though this was the last time we would ever see one another, as though to leave even a pair of earrings behind implied an unsustainable risk of dissolution.

3.   She talked often of dissolving, dissolving into the crowds pressing into her on the morning train, or dissolving into her family or office persona – and therefore by implication, of dissolving into her lover. It explained the importance of the bag, a symbol of freedom and independence, a desire for bracketing herself and recovering the parts she had dispersed in others.

4.   Yet whatever her efficiency with luggage, with time Chloe nevertheless began leaving things behind. Not toothbrushes or pairs of shoes, but pieces of herself. It began with language, with Chloe leaving me her way of saying *not ever* instead of *never*, and of stressing the *be* of *before*, or of saying *take care* before hanging up the telephone. She in turn acquired use of my *perfect* and *if you really think so*. Then habits began to leak between us; I acquired Chloe's need for total darkness in the bedroom, she followed my way of folding the newspaper, I took to wandering in circles around the sofa to think a problem through, she acquired a taste for lying on the carpet.

5.   Gradual diffusion brought with it a degree of intimacy, a state in which the borders between us ceased to be strictly patrolled, allowing a free passage for Brownian molecules. The body no longer felt the eyes of the other. Chloe would lie in bed reading and slide a finger into her nostril to clear an obstruction, rolling it into a ball till it was dry and hard, then swallowing it whole. Acquaintance with the body went beyond the sexual, we could lie together naked on a hot summer evening without reference to our nakedness. We could risk intervals of silence, we were no longer paranoid talkers, unwill-

ing to let the conversation drop lest tranquillity be unfaithful ['*What is s/he thinking of me in this silence?*']. We grew assured of ourselves in the other's mind, rendering perpetual seduction [the fear of its opposite] obsolete.

6.   With intimacy came a wealth of information on the *novelistic* as opposed to the *philosophic* aspect of existence: the smell of Chloe's skin after a shower, the sound of her voice while she spoke on the phone in the next room, the rumble of her stomach when she was hungry, her expression before a sneeze, the shape of her eyes when she awoke, the way she shook a wet umbrella, the sound of a brush through her hair.

7.   Aware of the other's characteristics, we acquired a need to rename one another. Love finds us with a name it did not invent, a name given to us by parents at birth and formalized by passports and civil registers. Given the uniqueness the lover locates, is it not natural it should find expression [however obliquely] in a name others do not use? Whereas in the office where she worked, Chloe was called Chloe, with me [and for reasons neither of us ever understood] she became known simply as *Tidge*. For my part, because I had once amused her with talk of the affliction of German intellectuals, I became known [perhaps less mysteriously] as *Weltschmerz*. The importance of these nicknames lay not in the particular name we had landed on – we might have ended up calling one another *Pwitt* and *Tic* – but in the fact we had chosen to relabel one another in the first place. *Tidge* suggested a knowledge of Chloe the bank clerk did not possess [the knowledge of her skin as she

emerged from the shower and the sound of a brush through her hair]. Whereas *Chloe* belonged to her civil status, *Tidge* lay beyond the political, in the more fluid and more unique realm of love. It was a victory over the past, a symbol of the re-christening and rebirth afforded by love. *I have found you with a given name*, says the lover, *but I am renaming you to label the difference between who you are to me, and who you are to others. You may be called X at the office [in political space] but in my bed, you will always be 'My Carrot'* . . .

8.   The play involved in nicknames spread to other areas of language. Whereas ordinary dialogue concerned itself with direct communication [hence with clear intentions], intimate language escaped the law, spared the need for an overt and constant *direction*. It could slide into illogicality and playfulness, into an expression of the stream of consciousness, abandoning Socratic logic for the carnivalesque, a voice rather than a communication. Love interpreted the tentative, what lay on the border between the said and unsaid, the expressible and inex-pressible [love as the will to extend understanding to the half-formulated thoughts of the other]. It was the difference between a doodle and an architectural drawing: the doodler has no need to know where the pencil is leading, the doodle surrenders like a kite; it was the freedom of not having a goal always in mind. We moved from dishwashers to Warhol to starch to nationality to projection to projectors to popcorn to penises to premature birth to infanticide to insecticide to sucking to flying to kissing. The censor of language was lifted, there were no Viennese slips because we were not standing up, lying in bed babbling through consciousness. Anything could

be said, it was a polyvalent cacophony of ideas. Authorship was freely surrendered, we swapped accents and ceded our own for those of politicians or pop stars, northerners or southerners. Unlike hard grammarians, we began a sentence unable to finish it, rescued from verbal insufficiency by the other, who would arrive to take up the slack and hang the pontoon on the next pillar.

9.   Intimacy did not destroy the self/other slash. It merely moved it outside the couple. Otherness now lay beyond the apartment door, confirming suspicions that love is never far from a conspiracy. Private judgements grew into a dual jury, the threats of the outside were shared on a common bed. In short, we gossiped. It was not always malicious, more the sorry outcome of an inability to remain ethical in ordinary interaction, hence creating a need to aerate accumulated lies. *It is because I cannot talk to you about this or that feature of your character [because you will not understand, or it will hurt you too much], that I will gossip/talk about it behind your back with someone else who will understand.* Chloe became the final repository of my judgements on the world. Things I had felt about friends or colleagues but could not have told them, things I had even tried to deny feeling about them, I was now free to share with Chloe. Love nourished itself by identifying common dislikes, *We both hate X* translated itself into *We like one another*. Lovers, hence criminals, our proof of loyalty became the extent to which we communicated our disloyalties towards others.

10.   Love may have been conspiratorial, but it was at least authentic. We retreated into each other's company to laugh at

the bad faith required by encounters with officialdom. We returned from formal dinners to mock the stiffness of the proceedings, imitating the accents and opinions of those to whom we had been politely saying goodbye minutes before. We would lie in bed and subvert the self-importance of upright life, replaying the polite question and answer volley of the dining ritual; I would ask Chloe the same questions as the bearded journalist had earlier asked her at table, she would answer them with the same politeness as she had used then, all this while she masturbated me beneath the sheets and I gently rubbed my leg up and down between her legs. Then suddenly, I would be shocked to find Chloe's hand where it was, would ask her in the haughtiest tones, *'Madam, what may I ask are you doing with my honourable member?'* *'My good sir,'* she would reply, *'the member's honourable behaviour is none of your business.'* Or Chloe would leap out of bed and say, *'Sir, please leave my bed immediately, you must have the wrong idea of me, we hardly know one another.'* In the space created by our intimacy, the formalities of upright life found themselves rerun in a comic light, like a tragedy that backstage is spoofed by the actors, the actor who plays Hamlet seizing Gertrude after the performance and shouting through the dressing-room, 'Fuck me, mother!'

11. But intimate time was not just lived and lost, it was converted into the story Chloe and I told ourselves about ourselves, the self-referential narrative of our love. With its roots in the epic tradition, love is necessarily tied to the tale [to speak of love always involves narrative], and more particularly, to adventure, structured by clear beginnings, endings, goals, reversals and triumphs. Day does not routinely follow day in

the epic, instead a teleology drives the characters forward – or the reader yawns and turns elsewhere. Paul and Virginie, Anna and Vronsky, Tarzan and Jane all struggle against odds that confirm and enrich their bond. Stranded in a jungle, on a shipwrecked boat or the side of a mountain, battling nature or society, epic couples prove the strength of their love by the vigour with which they overcome adversity.

12. With the modern love affair, the adventure loses its hegemony, what happens can no longer be a reflection of the character's inner states. Chloe and I were moderns, inner monologuers rather than adventurers. The world had been largely stripped of capacities for romantic struggle. The parents didn't care, the jungle had been tamed, society hid its disapproval behind universal tolerance, restaurants stayed open late, credit cards were accepted almost everywhere and sex was a duty, not a crime. And yet Chloe and I did have a story, a common history that would confirm our union [the weight of the past pressing down the often weightless present . . .].

13. It was not the stuff of thrillers, but its importance lay elsewhere, in allowing us to be bonded by a set of common experiences. What is an experience? Something that breaks a polite routine and for a brief period allows us to witness things with the heightened sensitivity afforded to us by novelty, danger, or beauty. To experience something is to fully open one's eyes in a way that habit prevents us from doing, and if two people open their eyes in this way at the same time, then we can expect them to be drawn together by it. Two people who are surprised by a lion in a jungle clearing will [if they

survive the experience] be triangularly bonded by what they have lived through.

Figure 13.1

14.   Chloe and I were never surprised by a lion, but we lived a host of small urban experiences. Returning from a party one night, we witnessed a dead body. The corpse lay on the corner of Charlwood Street and Belgrave Road. It was that of a woman who looked at first as though she had lain down on the pavement to sleep, perhaps because she was drunk. There was no blood or sign of a struggle, but as we were about to pass by, Chloe noticed the handle of a knife sticking out from the woman's stomach. How much does one know of someone till one has seen a corpse with them? We rushed over to the body, Chloe took on her nurse/schoolteacher voice, told me not to look, said we had to call the police, checked the woman's pulse [but she was indeed dead] and carefully left everything as she had found it. I was impressed by her professionalism, but in the middle of police questioning, she broke into uncontrollable sobbing and was unable to banish the image of the knife handle for several weeks. It was a horrific incident, but somehow it brought us closer together. We spent the rest of the night awake, drinking whisky in my apartment, and telling each other

a series of increasingly macabre and silly stories, impersonating corpses and policemen to exorcize our fears.

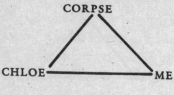

Figure 13.2

15.   A few months later, we were in a bagel shop in Brick Lane, when an elegant man in a pin-stripe suit next to us in the queue silently handed Chloe a crumpled note, on which was written in large scrawly letters the words: '*I love you.*' Chloe opened the piece of paper, swallowed hard on reading it, then looked back at the man who had given it to her. But he had chosen to act as though nothing had happened and simply stared out at the street with the dignified expression of a man in a pin-stripe suit. So just as innocently, Chloe folded the note and slipped it into her pocket. The bizarreness of the incident meant that, like the corpse only more light-heartedly, it became something of a leitmotif in our relationship, an incident in our story to which we alluded and over which we laughed. In restaurants, we would occasionally silently slip one another notes with all the mystery of the man in the bagel shop, but with only the message *Please pass the salt* written on them. For anyone watching, it must have seemed bizarre and incomprehensible to see us collapse into giggles. But this is the essence of leitmotifs, that they refer back to incidents others cannot understand for their absence in the founding scene. No wonder

such self-referential language annoys those standing on the sidelines.

16. The more familiar two people become, the more the language they speak together departs from that of ordinary, dictionary-defined discourse. Familiarity creates a new language, an *in-house* language of intimacy that carries references to the story the two lovers are weaving together, and that cannot readily be understood by others. It is a language alluding to their stock of shared experiences, it contains the history of the relationship, it is what makes talking to the loved one different from talking with anyone else.

17. There were many more joint incidents: people that we had encountered or things we had seen, done or heard and to which we would refer, comforted by our common heritage: there was the professor we met at a dinner who was writing a book claiming Freud's wife had been the true founder of psychoanalysis, there was my friend Will Knott with his often comic Californian habits, there was the toy giraffe we had bought in Bath to keep Chloe's elephant company on the bed, there was a meeting with an accountant on a train who confessed she always carried a gun in her handbag . . .

18. Interest did not naturally belong to such anecdotes: for the most part, only Chloe and I would understand, because of the subsidiary associations attached. Yet these leitmotifs were important because they gave us the feeling that we were not strangers to one another, that we had lived through something, and that we remembered the meaning we had jointly derived.

However slight these leitmotifs were, they acted like cement, the language of intimacy they helped create was a reminder that [without clearing our way through jungles, slaying dragons or sharing apartments] Chloe and I had created something of a world together.

CHAPTER FOURTEEN

'I'-CONFIRMATION

1.   Late one Sunday in the middle of July, we were sitting in a café on the Portobello Road. It had been a beautiful day, spent largely in Hyde Park, tanning and reading books. But since around five o'clock, I had been sliding into depression. I felt like going home to hide under the bedclothes, resisting only because there was nothing in particular to hide from. Sunday evenings had long saddened me, reminders of death, unfinished business, guilt and loss. We had been sitting in silence, Chloe reading the papers, I gazing through the window at the traffic and people outside. Suddenly she leaned over, gave me a kiss and whispered, 'You're wearing your lost orphan boy look again.' No one had ever ascribed such an expression to me before, though when Chloe mentioned it, it at once accorded with and alleviated the confused sadness I happened to be feeling at the time. I felt an intense [and perhaps disproportionate] love for her on account of that remark, because of her awareness of what I had been feeling but had been unable to formulate myself, for her willingness to enter my world and objectify it for me – a gratefulness for reminding the orphan he is an orphan, and hence returning him home.

2.   Perhaps it is true that we do not really exist until there is someone there to see us existing, we cannot properly speak until there is someone who can understand what we are saying, in essence, we are not wholly alive until we are loved.

3.   What does it mean that man is a 'social animal'? Only that humans need one another in order to define themselves and achieve self-consciousness, in a way that molluscs or earthworms do not. We cannot come to a proper sense of ourselves if there are not others around to show us where we end and others begin. 'A man can acquire anything in solitude except a character,' wrote Stendhal, suggesting that character has its genesis in the reactions of others to oneself. Because the 'I' is not an integrated structure, its fluidity requires the contours provided by others. I need another to help me carry my history, one who knows me as well, sometimes better, than I know myself.

4.   Without love, we lose the ability to possess a proper identity, within love, there is a constant confirmation of self. It is no wonder that the gaze of God is so important in religion: to be seen is to be assured existence, all the better if one is dealing with a God or partner who *loves* us. One's presence is legitimized in the eyes of another being who is for one [and for whom one is] the world. Surrounded by people who precisely do *not* remember who we are, people to whom we relate our histories on countless occasions and yet who will repeatedly forget how many times we have been married, how many children we have, and whether our name is Brad or Bill, Catrina or Catherine [and we forget much the same about them], is it not comforting to be able to find refuge from our

schizophrenia in the arms of someone who has our identity firmly in mind?

5.   It is no coincidence if, semantically speaking, love and interest are almost interchangeable, 'I love butterflies' meaning much the same as 'I am interested in butterflies'. To love someone is to take a deep interest in them, and hence by that concern, to bring them to a sense of what they are doing and saying. Through her understanding, Chloe's behaviour towards me gradually became studded with elements of what one could call '*I*'-*confirmation*. Contained in her intuitive understanding of many of my moods, in her knowledge of my tastes, in the things she told me about myself, in her memory of my routines and habits, and in her humorous acknowledgement of my phobias lay a multitude of these varied '*I*'-*confirmations* – the lover acting as a glove that returns the contours to the hand. Chloe noticed that I was a hypochondriac, that I was shy and hated speaking on the phone, was obsessive in my need to get eight hours' sleep a day, hated lingering in restaurants at the end of meals, used politeness as an aggressive defence, and preferred to say 'maybe' rather than yes or no. She would quote me back at myself ['*Last time, you said you didn't like that kind of irony . . .*'], demonstrating a grasp of my character by holding in mind elements – both good and bad – of my story ['*You always panic whenever . . .' 'I've never seen anyone forget petrol as often as you do . . .*'] I was involved in a process of maturation, arising out of the deeper insights into myself that Chloe's presence afforded. It takes the intimacy of a lover to point out facets of character others simply do not bother with, sides that it may be difficult to confront. There were times when Chloe would tell me quite

frankly that I was being defensive, or critical, or hostile or jealous or pathetically childish or any number of negative [but true] things – moments when I would be brought face to face with areas of myself that ordinary introspection [in the interests of inner harmony] would have avoided, that others would have been too uninterested to highlight, and that it took the honesty of the bedroom to reveal.

6.   Love seems bounded by two dissolutions – that of living under too many eyes, and that of living under too few. Chloe had always felt the former to be the greater danger. Suffocated in childhood, she had seen adulthood as a chance to escape the stiffness others' eyes conferred to her movements. She had dreamt of living alone in the country, in a spacious white house with large windows and scarcely any furniture, a symbol of escape from a world whose oppressive gaze exhausted her. When she was nineteen, she had tried to realize her desire by travelling to Arizona, where she settled in a cabin on the edge of a small town where she knew no one, thousands of miles from home. Imbued with a youthful romanticism, she had taken a suitcase full of the classics with her, which she intended to read and annotate as she watched the sun rise and set over the desert moonscape. But within a few weeks of arriving, she began to feel the solitude she had longed for all her life disorientating, frightening, unreal. The sound of her own voice came as a shock when she heard it every week at the minimarket, she took to staring at herself in the mirror to retain a sense of being, of her borders. Finally, after only a month, she left the town for a job as a waitress in a restaurant in Phoenix, unable to bear any longer the 'unreality' that had descended on her.

When she reached Phoenix, social contact came as an enormous shock. She found herself unable to answer such basic questions as what she had been doing. She had lost all sense of being an 'I', the experiences she had had seemed unable to be formulated in language.

7. If love returns us our reflection, then solitude is like being denied the use of a mirror, and allowing one's imagination to make what it will of a cut or spot we know we have on our face. Whatever the damage, at least the mirror returns us a sense of ourselves, gives us a clear outline with which we may answer the boundlessness of our imagination. Because a sense of who we are is not self-generated, fuzziness accompanied Chloe in the desert, the outlines of her character blurring away from the focus of others, her imagination taking hold of her and expanding her into a monstrous creature, swollen with the paranoias and delusions it may engender. The reaction of others to our conduct is comparable to a mirror because it throws back an image of ourselves *we ourselves are not able to see*. It is what makes others so indispensable, that they are able to give us something we are unable to grasp alone, the elusive sense of our borders, the sense of our own character. Who am I without others to hint at an answer? [Who was I without Chloe to hint at the right answer?]

8. It was a long time before I was able to grasp Chloe as a *character*, before I began to see what part she played in her own story, the story she told herself about her own life. Only slowly did I begin to unearth, from among the millions of words she spoke and actions her body performed, the structuring threads

that ran through her, the points of connection that could contain her multiplicities. In our knowledge of others, we are necessarily made to interpret a whole from parts. To fully know someone, one would in theory have to spend every minute of their life with them, within them. Failing this, we are left as detectives and analysts [psycho-detectives] piecing together wholes from clues. But we always arrive too late, after the crime/ primal-scene has been committed, and are hence forced to slowly reconstruct a past from its sediment, like analysing a dream after we have awoken.

9.   Understanding Chloe, I was like a doctor passing hands over a body, trying to intuit the interior. I was forced to work on the surface while trying to sound the depths, attempting to connect why a sudden bad mood or violent hatred or joy had arisen, what this would tell me of who Chloe was. But it all took time and there was always a sense of reaching the scene too late, of running to catch up with a moving target. To give an example, it took a while before I understood the characteristic importance of Chloe's inclination to suffer alone rather than disturb others. One morning, Chloe told me she had been violently ill in the night, had even driven to an all-night chemist, and yet had all the while been careful not to wake me up. My first reaction was bewildered anger – why had she not said something? Was our relationship really so distant that she could not even wake me up in a crisis? But my anger [only a form of jealousy] was crude, it failed to take into account what I would only gradually learn, namely how deep seated and pervasive a feature of Chloe's character it was to load blame on herself, to

tear herself apart instead of fighting back, or waking anyone up. She would had to have been near death before waking me, for everything about her wished not to load responsibility on others. Once I had located this strand in her nature, a hundred different aspects of her could be understood as a manifestation of it – her lack of knowledgeable anger towards her parents [an anger that allowed itself expression only in savage irony], her immense dedication to work, her self-deprecation, her harshness towards self-pitying people, her sense of duty, even her way of crying [muted sobs rather than hysterical wailing].

10. Like a telephone engineer, I identified the dominant strands in the spaghetti jumble of a self in motion: I began recognizing her hatred of stinginess every time we were in a group in a restaurant, her willingness to pay for everyone rather than watch a fight over money. I began sensing her desire not to be trapped, the desert-escapist side of her nature. I admired her constant visual creativity which showed not just in her work, but in the way she would lay the table or arrange a bowl of flowers. I began detecting her awkwardness with other women and her greater ease with men. I recognized her fierce loyalty to those she considered her friends, an instinctive sense of clan and community. With such characteristics, Chloe slowly came to assume coherence in my mind, someone with consistency and a degree of predictability, someone whose tastes in a film or a person I could now begin to guess without asking.

11. But acting as a mirror for Chloe was not always easy. Unlike the real object, the metaphorical mirror can never be

143

passive. It is an active mirror that must *find* the image of the other, it is a searching, roving mirror, one that seeks to capture the dimensions of a moving shape, the incredible complexity of another's character. It is a hand mirror, and the hand that holds it is not a steady one, for it has its own interests and concerns – is the image one wishes to find really the one that exists? *What do you see in her?* the mind asks the mirror: *What do you want to see in her?* the heart asks the mirror.

12.   The danger of *'I'-confirmation* is that we need others to legitimate our existence, but are thereby at their mercy to have a correct identity ascribed to us. If, as Stendhal says, we lack a character without others, then the other with whom we share our bed must be a skilled reflector – or we will end up deformed. What if we are loved by people with the grossest misunderstandings, those who deny us a side of ourselves by the poverty of their empathy? And what of the greater doubt: do not others by definition [because the mirrored surface is never smooth] distort us, whether for the better or for the worse?

13.   Everyone returns us to a different sense of ourselves, for we become a little of who they think we are. One could compare the self to an amoeba, whose outer walls are elastic, and therefore adapt to the environment. It is not that the amoeba has no *dimensions*, simply that it has no self-defined *shape*. It is my absurdist side that an absurdist person will draw out of me, but it is my seriousness that a serious person will evoke. If someone thinks I am shy, I will probably end up shy, if someone thinks me funny, I am likely to keep cracking jokes. The process is circular:

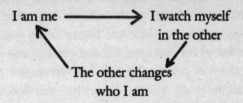

Figure 14.1

14.   Chloe had lunch with my parents: she was silent through-out the entire meal. When we returned home, I asked her what was wrong. She herself couldn't understand. She had tried to be lively and interesting and yet the suspicions of the two strangers facing her across the table had stopped her from expanding into her usual self. My parents had done nothing overtly wrong, yet something about them had prevented her from rising above monosyllability. It was a reminder that the labelling of others is not a violently obvious process. Most people do not force us into roles, they merely suggest them by their reactions, and hence ever so gently prevent us moving beyond the assigned mould.

15.   A few years before, Chloe had for a time been seeing an academic at London University. The analytical philosopher, who had written five books and contributed to many scholarly journals, had left her with a legacy – an unwarranted sense of total mental inadequacy. How had he done this? Again, Chloe could not tell. Without ever using precise language to do so, he had succeeded in shaping the amoeba according to his precon-

145

ceptions – namely, that Chloe was a beautiful young student who should leave matters of the mind to him. And so, like a self-fulfilling prophecy, Chloe had begun acting unconsciously on the verdict of her character, handed out like an end of term report by the wise philosopher who had written five books and contributed to many scholarly journals. She had ended up feeling exactly as stupid as she was told.

16. Chronology means the child is always narrated from a third-person perspective [*'Isn't Chloe a cute/ugly/intelligent/stupid kid?'*], before it gains the ability to influence its own narration. Overcoming childhood could be understood as an attempt to correct the false narrations of others, of our story-telling parents. But the struggle against narration continues beyond childhood: a propaganda war surrounds the decision of who we are, a number of interest groups struggling to assert their view of reality, to have their story heard. Yet reality remains distorted – either out of an enemy's jealousy, or the indifferent's neglect or our own egocentric blindness. Even to love someone implies a gross preconception, a decision taken that someone is a genius or the most beautiful person on earth on the basis of not very much at all, an approach very far removed from the neutral stance real understanding might call for – a pleasant distortion, but a distortion nevertheless. Looking to confirm ourselves in another's eyes is like looking in fun-fair mirrors: the tiny person suddenly appears three metres tall, the thin woman becomes enormous, the fat one, slim, we develop a giraffe neck or elephant feet, a bad character or a saint's one, a large brain or a tiny one, long beautiful legs or no legs at all. Like Narcissus, we are doomed to a certain disappointment in gazing at our

reflection in the watery eyes of another. *No eye can wholly contain our 'I'.* We will always be chopped off in some area or other, fatally or not.

17.   When I told Chloë about this idea that character was a bit like an amoeba, she laughed and told me she'd loved drawing amoebas at school. Then she took up a pencil.

'Here, give me the newspaper, I'll draw you the difference between what shape my amoeba-self has at the office and what shape it has with you.'

Then she drew the following:

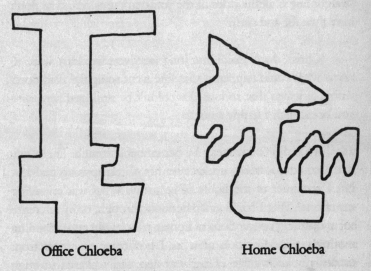

Office Chloeba   Home Chloeba

Figure 14.2

'What are all the wiggly bits?' I asked.
'Oh, that's because I feel wiggly around you.'

'What?'

'Well, you know, you give me space. I feel more complicated than in the office. You're interested in me and you
understand me better, so that's why I made it wiggly, so that
it's sort of natural.'

'OK, I see, so what's this straight side?'

'Where?'

'Up in the north-east of the amoeba.'

'You know I never got geography O-level. But yeah, I
think I see it. Well, you don't understand *everything* about me,
do you? So I thought I'd better make it more realistic. The
straight line is all the sides of me you don't understand or don't
have time for and stuff.'

'Oh.'

'Christ, don't make that long face, you wouldn't want to
know what could happen if that line went squiggly! And don't
worry, if it was that serious, I wouldn't be squidged here with
you being such a happy amoeba.'

18.   What did Chloe mean by her amoebic straight line? Only
that I could not *wholly* understand her – unsurprising perhaps,
but a reminder of the limits of empathy. What was curtailing
my efforts? That I could grasp her only through, or by reference
to, my existing conceptions of human nature. My understanding
was only a modification of what I had come to expect from
others, my knowledge of her was necessarily filtered through
my past social interactions. Like a European who orients himself
in a Rocky Mountain landscape by saying, 'This looks just like
Switzerland,' I might only be able to grasp the source of one of
Chloe's depressed moods by thinking, 'It's because she's feeling

x . . . like my sister when . . .' All my experience of women and men was used to comprehend her – my whole, very subjective and hence distorted understanding of human nature was brought into play, dependent on my biology, class, country, and psychobiography.

19.   One could compare a lover's gaze to a barbecue skewer. Within the complexity of our nature, every lover picks up on certain elements and neglects others: my gaze for instance picked up on [or appreciated or understood or related to] Chloe's:

> > *— irony — colour of eyes — gap between two front teeth — intellect — talent for baking bread — relationship with her mother — social anxiety — love of Beethoven — hatred of laziness — taste for camomile tea — objection to snobbery — love of woollen clothes — claustrophobia — desire for honesty —* >

But it was not the whole of her. Had this been a different barbecue skewer and I a different lover, I might have had more time for her:

> > *— interest in healthy eating — ankles — love of outdoor markets — mathematical talent — relationship with her brother — love of nightclubs — thoughts on God — enthusiasm for rice — Degas — skating — long country walks — objection to music in the car — taste for Victorian architecture —* >

149

20.   Though I had felt myself attentive to the complexities of Chloe's nature, there were necessarily moments of great abbreviation, areas which I simply did not have the empathy or maturity to understand. I was guilty of the most unavoidable but greatest abbreviation of all, that of only being able to participate in Chloe's life as an outsider, whose inner life I could imagine, but never directly experience. We were divided by the I/you polarity, the I and non-I. However close we might be, Chloe was in the end *another human being*, with all the mystery and distance this implies [the inevitable distance embodied in the thought that we must die alone . . .].

21.   We long for a love without straight borders or straight lines, a love in which we are not reduced. We have a morbid resistance to classification by others, to others placing labels on us [the man, the woman, the rich one, the poor one, the Jew, the Catholic, etc.]. Our objection is not so much that these labels are untrue as that they fail to accurately reflect the subjective sense of unclassifiability. To ourselves, we are after all always *un-labelable*. When alone, we are always simply 'me' and shift between labelled parts effortlessly and without the constraint imposed by the preconceptions of others. Hearing Chloe once talk of '*this guy I was seeing a few years ago*', I was suddenly saddened, imagining myself in a few years time [another man facing her across the tuna salad] described as '*this guy I was seeing a while ago . . .*' Her casual reference to a past lover provided the necessary objectification for me to realize that, however special I might have been to her at the time, I still existed within certain definitions ['a guy', 'a boyfriend'], that I

was [however much of a special one] nothing more than a reflection in Chloe's eyes.

22.   But as we must be labelled, characterized and defined by others, the person we end up loving is by definition the *good enough barbecue skewerer*, the person who loves us for more or less the things we deem ourselves lovable for, who understands us for more or less the things we need to be understood for. That Chloeba and I were together implied that for the moment at least, we had been given enough room to expand in the ways our inherent fluidity demanded.

CHAPTER FIFTEEN

INTERMITTENCES
OF THE HEART

1. Language flatters our indecisions with its stability. It allows us to hide under an illusory permanence and fixity while the world changes minute by minute. 'No man steps into the same river twice,' said Heraclitus, pointing to the inevitable flux yet ignoring the fact that if the *word* for river does not change, then in an important sense, it is the same river we appear to have stepped into. I was a man in love with a woman, but how much of the mobility and inconstancy of my emotions could such words hope to carry? Was there room in them for all the infidelity, boredom, irritation, and indifference that often found themselves knitted together with this love? Could any words hope to accurately reflect the degree of ambivalence to which my emotions seemed fated?

2. I call myself a name, and the name stays with me throughout my life – the 'I' that I see in a picture of myself at the age of six and that I will perhaps see in a picture of myself at sixty will both be framed by the same letters, though time will have altered me almost unrecognizably. I call a tree a tree, though throughout the year, the tree changes. To rename the tree at every season would be too confusing, so language settles on the

152

continuity, forgetting that in one season there are leaves that in another will be absent.

3.   We hence proceed by abbreviation, we take the dominant feature [of a tree, of an emotional state] and label as the whole something that is only a part. Similarly, the story we tell of an event remains a segment of the totality the moment comprised; as soon as the moment is narrated, it loses its multiplicity and ambivalence in the name of abstracted meaning and authorial intent. The story embodies the poverty of the remembered moment. Chloe and I lived a love story stretching over an expanse of time during which my feelings moved so far across the emotional scale that to talk of being simply *in love* seems a brutal foreshortening of events. Pressed for time and eager to simplify, we are forced to narrate and remember things by ellipsis, or we would be overwhelmed by both our ambivalence and our instability. The present becomes degraded, first into history, then into nostalgia.

4.   Chloe and I spent a pleasant weekend in Bath together. We visited the Roman baths, we had dinner in an Italian restaurant, and took a walk around the crescents on Sunday afternoon. What remains of this weekend in Bath? A few mental photographs – the purple curtains of the room in which we slept, the view of the city from the train, a park, a clock above a mantelpiece. These are the pictorial remains. The emotional ones are even sketchier. I remember being happy, I remember loving Chloe. And yet if I force myself to think back, to rely on more than immediate memory, then I recall a more complicated

history: frustration at the crowds in the museum, anxiety on going to sleep on Saturday night, slight indigestion after a veal escalope, an annoying delay at Bath train station, an argument with Chloe in the taxi.

5.   Perhaps we can forgive language its hypocrisy because it enables us to recall a weekend in Bath with one word, *pleasant*, hence creating a manageable order and identity. Yet at times one is brought face to face with the flux beneath the word, the water flowing beneath Heraclitus's *river* – and one longs for the simplicity things assume when letters are the only guardians of their borders. I loved Chloe – how easy it sounds, like someone saying they love apple juice or Marcel Proust. And yet how much more complex the reality was, so complex that I struggle against saying anything conclusive of any one moment, for to say one thing is automatically to miss out on another – every assertion symbolizing the repression of a thousand counter-assertions.

6.   When her friend Alice invited us to dinner one Friday night, Chloe accepted and predicted I would fall in love with her. There were eight of us around Alice's dining table, everyone jogging elbows as they tried to bring the food to their mouths over a table built for four. Alice lived alone in the top floor of a house in Balham, worked as a secretary at the Arts Council, and I had to admit; I did fall a little in love with her.

7.   However happy we may be with our partner, our love for them necessarily prevents us [unless we live in a polygamous society] from starting other romantic liaisons. But why should

this constrain us if we truly loved them? Why should we feel this as a loss unless our love for them has already begun to wane? The answer perhaps lies in the uncomfortable thought that in resolving our need to love, we may not always succeed in resolving our need to long.

8.   Watching Alice talk, light a candle that had blown out, rush into the kitchen with the plates and brush a strand of blonde hair from her face, I found myself falling victim to romantic nostalgia. Romantic nostalgia descends when we are faced with those who might have been our lovers, but whom chance has decreed we will never know. The possibility of an alternative love life is a reminder that the life we are leading is only one of a myriad of possible lives: and it is perhaps the impossibility of leading them all that plunges us into sadness. There is a longing for a return to a time without the need for choices, free of the sadness at the inevitable loss that all choice [however wonderful] has entailed.

9.   In city streets or busy restaurants, I would often be made aware of hundreds [and by implication even millions] of women whose lives were running concurrently with mine, but who were doomed to remain a mystery to me. Though I loved Chloe, the sight of these women occasionally filled me with regret. Standing on a train platform or in line at the bank, I would catch sight of a given face, perhaps overhear a snatch of conversation [someone's car had broken down, someone was graduating from university, a mother was ill . . .], and feel momentary sadness at being unable to know the rest of the story, consoling myself by inventing a narrative that might fit.

10.   I could have talked to Alice on the sofa after dinner, but something made me reluctant to do anything but dream. Alice's face evoked a void inside of me with no clear dimensions or intentions and that my love for Chloe had somehow not resolved. The unknown carries with it a mirror of all our deepest, most inexpressible wishes. The unknown is the fatal proposition that a face seen across the room will always hold out to the known. I may have loved Chloe but because I *knew* Chloe, I did not *long* for her. Longing cannot indefinitely direct itself at those we know, for their qualities are charted and therefore lack the mystery longing demands. A face seen for a few moments or hours only then to disappear for ever is the necessary catalyst for dreams that cannot be formulated, an empty space, an immeasurable desire within oneself that seems as undefinable as it is unquenchable.

11.   'So, did you fall in love with her?' Chloe asked in the car.
      'Of course not.'
      'She's your type.'
      'No, she isn't. And anyway, you know I'm in love with you.'
      In the typical scenario of betrayal, one partner asks the other, 'How could you have betrayed me with *x* when you said you loved *me*?' But there is no inconsistency between a betrayal and a declaration of love if time is taken into the equation. 'I love you' can only ever be taken to mean, 'I love you *now*.' I was not lying to Chloe by telling her I loved her on the way back home from Alice's dinner party, but my words had only ever been time-bound promises.

12. If my feelings towards Chloe changed, it was in part because she herself was not an unalterable being, but a perpetually shifting nexus of meaning. The constancy of her job and telephone number was an illusion, or rather, a simplification. To an attentive eye, her face registered the minutest changes in her psychological and physiological condition, one could notice her accent altering according to who she was with or what film she had seen, her shoulders fell when she was tired, her height increased with her self-esteem. There was her face as it looked on a Monday and on a Friday, her eyes when she felt sad and when she was aroused, the veins on her hand when she read the paper and when she was in the shower. There was her face from a dozen angles, across a table, pressing close before a kiss or on a train platform. There was Chloe with her parents, and Chloe with her lover, Chloe smiling, and Chloe flossing her teeth.

13. I would have needed to be a limitless biographer to chart these changes; instead I was a lazy creature of habit. Exhaustion often meant letting the richest part of Chloe's life – her movement – slip by. I would for long periods cease to *notice* [because she had grown familiar] all the mutations coursing through her body or the lines sketched over her face, the difference in Chloe on a Monday and on a Friday. The idea of her became a habit, a stable image in the mind's eye.

14. Yet there would come moments when the smooth surface of habit would rupture, and once more I would be allowed to look properly at her, with the eyes of someone who had never seen her before. One weekend, we broke down on the

motorway and had to call for help. When an AA van stopped a quarter of an hour later, Chloe went to deal with the officer. Watching her talk to a stranger [by a form of identification with him] the woman I knew suddenly appeared foreign to me. I looked at her face and heard her voice without the dulling blanket of familiarity, I saw her as she would be to someone who had never laid eyes on her, rather than as she had come to be for me, I saw her stripped of the preconceptions time had imposed.

15.   And suddenly, watching her talk of spark plugs and oil filters, I was filled with uncontrollable desire. The disruption of habit had had an estrangement effect, making Chloe unknown and exotic – and hence desirable with the intensity of someone whose body one had never touched. It took the AA man only a few minutes to locate the fault, something to do with the battery, then we were ready to continue to London. But my desire signalled otherwise.

'We have to stop, go to a hotel or park in a country lane. We have to make love.'

'Why? What's wrong? What are you doing? Please, not now, my God . . . ohhhh, Christ, don't . . . Hhhhmmmm, OK, wait, we'd better stop the car, let's turn off here . . .'

16.   The attraction of Chloe-as-stranger was a reminder of the relation between movement and sexuality, namely, the movement from the dressed to the undressed body. We stopped in a lane just off the M4. My hand reached to caress her breasts through the light fabric of her dress, the erotic emerging from the return to what had been estranged, the body lost and

regained. It was an ecstatic interval between nakedness and dress, the familiar and the unfamiliar, a transgression and initiation.

17.   We made love twice on the back seat of Chloe's Volkswagen, in between pieces of luggage and old papers. But though welcome, our sudden and unpredictable desire, the grasping at one another's clothes and flesh, was a reminder of how destructive the flux of passions might be. Seized off the motorway by desire, might we not similarly drift apart on the back of another hormone at a later date? It was perhaps implying an unrealistic degree of logic to have called our emotions cyclical. Our love seemed more like the turbulent flow of a mountain stream than the gentle shift of seasons.

18.   Chloe and I had a joke between us, a Heraclitean practice that acknowledged the fluctuation of our emotions, and eased the common-sensist demand that love's light burn with the constancy of an electric bulb.

'Is something wrong? Do you not like me today?' one of us would ask.

'I like you less.'

'Really, much less?'

'No, not that much.'

'Out of ten?'

'Today? Oh, probably six and a half or, no, perhaps more six and three-quarters. And how about with you with me?'

'God, I'd say around minus three, though it might have been around twelve and a half earlier this morning when you . . .'

19. In another Chinese restaurant [Chloe loved them], I realized that encounters with others were perhaps much like the circular wheel at the centre of the table, on which dishes were placed and could be revolved so one would be faced by shrimp one minute, by pork the next. Did loving someone not follow the same circular pattern, in which good and bad revolved in time? Otherwise mobile, we remain mistakenly attached to the fixity of human emotions, and to the idea of a hermetic division between love and non-love, one that should be crossed only twice, at the beginning and end of a relationship – rather than commuted across daily, or hourly. There is an impulse to split love and hate apart rather than see them as legitimate responses to the many sides of a single person. There is a childish need to love the wholly good and hate the wholly bad, to find a single unquestionably apt target for either one's aggressive or loving instincts. But there could be no such stability with Chloe. It would only require an instant for me to revolve through every dish on her Chinese platter, dizzy at the confusion implied. I might feel she was:

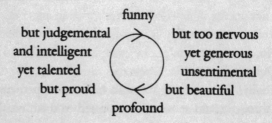

Figure 16.1

160

20.   It was often hard to know what set the wheel spinning from one emotion to another. I might see Chloe sitting in a certain way, or saying a certain thing, and be suddenly intensely irritated by her, when only a short time before it had all been sweetness and light. I was not alone, for there were times when Chloe too would display bursts of aggression against me. Discussing a film with friends one night, she abruptly launched into a hostile speech about my patronizing attitudes towards other people's tastes and opinions. I was at first baffled, for I had not yet said anything, but I guessed that something I had done earlier must have upset her, and that she was now using this opportunity to vent her frustration – or else that someone else had upset her, and that I was standing in for a currently absent target. Many of our arguments had this quality of unfairness, in the sense that they were excuses for expressing feelings that did not belong to the present moment or indeed to either of us. I might get furious with Chloe not for the surface reason that she was emptying the dishwasher very noisily when I was trying to watch the news, but because I was feeling anxious and guilty about not answering a difficult business call earlier in the day. Chloe might in turn have been deliberately making lots of noise in an effort to symbolize an anger she had not communicated to me that morning. [We could perhaps define maturity – that ever-elusive goal – as the ability to give everyone what they deserve when they deserve it, to separate the emotions that belong and should be restricted to oneself from those that should at once be expressed to their initiators, rather than passed on to later and more innocent arrivals.]

21.   One may wonder why those who claim to love us at the same time harbour such apparently unfair hostilities and resentments. We shelter within us an untold number of contradictory emotions, broad layers of infantile responses over which we can have little or no control. Rages, cannibalistic urges, destructive fantasies, bisexualities, and childhood paranoias are all enmeshed within the more respectable emotions. 'We should never say people are evil,' wrote the French philosopher Alain, 'we should just look for the needle' – that is, look for the irritant that lies behind an argument or aggression. Chloe and I were well disposed to try, but the complexities were at times overwhelming, everything from the vagaries of sexual impulses to the influences of childhood traumas.

22.   If philosophers have traditionally advocated a life lived according to reason, condemning in its name a life led by desires, it is because reason is the bedrock of continuity, it has no time-bound dimension, no sell-by date. Unlike the romantic, the philosopher does not for instance let his or her interest veer insanely from Chloe to Alice to Chloe, because stable reasons support any choice made. In their desires, philosophers will witness only evolutions, not ruptures. In love, they will stay faithful and constant, their life as assured as the trajectory of an arrow in flight.

23.   But more importantly, the philosopher will be assured an *identity*. What is identity? Perhaps it is shaped around what a person is disposed towards: *I am what I like*. *Who I am* is to a large extent constituted by *what I want*. If I have loved golf since the age of ten, and am now a hundred and twenty and still

love the sport, then my identity [both as a golfer and indirectly as a person] has proved a stable one. If I maintain a faith in Catholicism from the age of two to the age of ninety, I am able to avoid the identity crisis of the Jew who wakes up at thirty-five with a wish to become a bishop or the pope who at the end of his life converts to Islam.

24.   Life for the emotional is very different, comprised of dizzying revolutions of the clock, for *what they want* changes so rapidly that *who they are* is constantly in question. If the emotional man one day loves Samantha and the next Sally, then who is he? If I went to bed one night loving Chloe, and awoke the next morning hating her, then *who* was 'I'? I did not wholly give up on the project of becoming a more reasonable person. I was simply faced with the intractable problem of locating solid *reasons* for either loving or not-loving Chloe. Objectively, there were no compelling reasons to do either, which made my occasional ambivalence towards her all the more unresolvable. Had there been sound, unassailable [dare I say logical] reasons to love or hate, there would have been benchmarks to return to. But much as the gap between her two front teeth had never been a reason to fall head over heels in love with her, could I really have cited her way of scratching her elbow as the basis for hatred? Whatever the reasons we may consciously cite, we are never more than partially aware of the basis of our attraction [*and hence the irreversible and tragic process falling out of love implies* . . .]

25.   Opposed to the discontinuities, there was a natural homoeostatic urge: *the maintenance of the constancy of the emotional*

163

environment. The homoeostatic impulse moderated fluctuations, aimed for stability and avoidance of turbulence, desired continuity and coherence. Homoeostasis anchored me to a linear love story, that of Chloe and I, reining me in when there might have been an urge to develop sub-plots, to digress from or question my story with the schizophrenia of modern fiction. Upon waking up from an erotic dream spent with a blend of two faces seen in a shop the day before, I at once relocated myself on finding Chloe beside me. I stereotyped my possibilities, I returned to the role assigned to me by my story, I bowed to the tremendous authority of what already exists.

26.   Fluctuations were kept in check by the continuities of the environment, by the more stable assumptions of those around us. I remember a furious row that erupted a few minutes before we were due to meet friends for coffee one Saturday. At the time, we both felt this row to be so serious we might have broken up over it. Yet the possibility of ending the story was curtailed by friends who could envisage no such thing. Over coffee, there were questions directed at the happy couple, questions betraying no knowledge of the possibility of rupture and hence helping to avoid it. The presence of others moderated our swings, when we were unsure of what we wanted and hence who we were, we could hide under the comforting analysis of those who stood on the outside, aware only of the continuities, unaware that there was nothing inviolable about our plot line.

27.   In our better moods, we would also find comfort under the illusion of a projected future. Because there was a threat that love would end as suddenly as it had begun, it was natural

that we should reinforce the present with an appeal to a common future, one lasting at the very least until our death. We dreamt of where we would live, how many children we would have, what pension scheme we would adopt, we identified ourselves with the oldies taking their grandchildren for walks and holding hands in Kensington Gardens. Defending ourselves against love's demise, we took pleasure in planning our lives together on a grandiose time scale. There were houses we both liked near Notting Hill and together decorated in our heads, completing them with two small studies at the top, a large fitted kitchen with the sleekest appliances in the basement, and a garden full of flowers and trees. Though things were never likely to proceed that far, *we had to believe there was no reason why they should not*. How is it possible to love someone and at the same time imagine separating from them, marrying and decorating a house with someone else? No, it was indispensable for us to contemplate what it would be like to grow old together and retire with our dentures to a bungalow by the sea. Had we believed in it, we might even have planned to marry, that most ruthless of legal attempts to force the heart into endless love.

28. My dislike of talking about ex-lovers with Chloe was perhaps part of the same phenomenon of wanting things to last for ever. These ex-lovers were reminders that situations I had at one point thought to be permanent had proved not to be so, and that my relationship with Chloe might undergo a similar fate. One evening, in the bookshop of the Hayward Gallery, I caught sight of an old girlfriend, leafing through a book on Picasso by a shelf across the room. Chloe was a few steps away from me, searching for some postcards to send to friends.

Picasso had meant much to this ex-girlfriend and me. I could easily have gone to say hello. I had after all met several of Chloe's former lovers, many of whom she saw on a regular basis. But the discomfort was in me: it was simply that this woman was a reminder of a fickleness in my emotions I preferred to avoid. I feared that the intimacy I had created with her and then lost might prove a pattern repeated with Chloe.

29.   The tragedy of love is that it does not escape the temporal dimensions. When one is with a current lover, there is a particular cruelty in the thought of one's indifference towards past loves. There is something appalling in the idea that the person for whom you would sacrifice anything for today might in a few months cause you to cross the road [or bookshop] to avoid them. I realized that if my love for Chloe constituted the essence of my self at that moment, then the definitive end of my love for her would mean nothing less than the death of a part of me.

30.   If Chloe and I continued despite all this to believe we were in love, it was perhaps because, in the end, the moments of love far outweighed [for a time at least] the moments of boredom or indifference. Yet we always remained aware that what we had chosen to call love might be an abbreviation for a far more complex, and ultimately less palatable, reality.

CHAPTER SIXTEEN

THE FEAR OF HAPPINESS

1.   One of love's greatest drawbacks is that, for a while at least, it is in danger of making us happy.

2.   Chloe and I chose to travel to Spain in the final week of August – travel [like love] an attempt to follow a dream into reality. In London, we had read the brochures of Utopia Travel, specialists in the Spanish rental market, and had settled for a converted farm house in the village of Aras de Alpuente, in the mountains behind Valencia. The house looked better in reality than it had in the photographs. The rooms were simply but comfortably furnished, the bathroom worked, there was a terrace shaded by vine leaves, a lake near by to swim in and a farmer next door who kept a goat and welcomed us with a gift of olive oil and cheese.

3.   We had arrived in the late afternoon, having hired a car at the airport and driven up the narrow mountain roads. We immediately went for a swim, diving into the clear blue waters and drying off in the dying sun. Then we had returned to the house and sat on the terrace with a bottle of wine and olives to watch the sun set behind the hills.

    'Isn't it wonderful,' I remarked lyrically.

'Isn't it?' echoed Chloe.

'But is it?' I joked.

'Shush, you're ruining the scene.'

'No, I'm serious, it really is wonderful. I could never have imagined a place like this existing. It seems so cut off from everything, like a paradise no one's bothered to ruin.'

'I could spend the rest of my life here,' sighed Chloe.

'So could I.'

'We could live here together, I'd tend the goats, you'd handle the olives, we'd write books, paint and fa . . .'

'Are you all right?' I asked, seeing Chloe suddenly wince with pain.

'Yeah, I am now. I don't know what happened. I just got this terrible pain in my head, like an awful throbbing or something. It's probably nothing. Ah, no, shit, there it comes again.'

'Let me feel.'

'You won't be able to feel anything, it's inside.'

'I know, but I'll empathize.'

'God, I'd better lie down. It's probably just the travelling, or the height, or something. But I'd better go inside. You stay out here, I'll be fine.'

4. Chloe's pains did not get better. She took an aspirin and went to bed, but was unable to sleep. Unsure of how seriously to take her suffering, but worried her natural tendency to play things down meant it was probably more serious than it seemed, I decided to get a doctor. The farmer and his wife were in their cottage eating dinner when I knocked and asked in fragments of Spanish where the nearest doctor could be found. It turned

out helived in Villar del Arzobispo, a village some twenty kilometres away.

5.   Dr Saavedra was immensely dignified for a country doctor. He wore a white linen suit, had spent a term at Imperial College in the 1950s, was a lover of the English theatrical tradition and seemed delighted to accompany me back to assist the maiden who had fallen ill so early in her Spanish sojourn. When we arrived back in Aras de Alpuente, Chloe's condition was no better. I left the doctor alone with her and waited nervously in the next room. Ten minutes later, the doctor emerged.

'Ess nutting to worry about.'

'She'll be OK?'

'Yes, my friend, she'll be OK in the mornin'.'

'What was wrong with her?'

'Nutting much, a leetle stomach, a leetle head, ees very common among dee 'oliday makres. I give her peels. Really just a little anch-edonia in de head, wha you espect?'

6.   Dr Saavedra had diagnosed a case of *anhedonia*, a disease defined by the British Medical Association as a reaction remarkably close to mountain sickness resulting from the sudden terror brought on by the threat of happiness. It was a common disease among tourists in this region of Spain, faced in these idyllic surroundings with the sudden realization that earthly happiness might be within their grasp, and prey therefore to a violent physiological reaction designed to counteract such a possibility.

7.   The problem with happiness is that in its rarity, it proves intensely terrifying and anxiety-inducing to accept. Hence,

somewhat unconsciously, Chloe and I [though I had not fallen ill] had always tended to locate *hedonia* either in memory or in anticipation. Though the pursuit of happiness was an avowed central goal, it was accompanied by an implicit belief in the realization of this Aristotelianism somewhere in the very distant future – a belief challenged by the idyll we had found in Aras de Alpuente and, to a lesser extent, in each other's arms.

8.   Why did we live this way? Perhaps because to enjoy ourselves in the present would have meant engaging ourselves in an imperfect or dangerously ephemeral reality, rather than hiding behind a comfortable belief in an after-life. Living in the *future perfect tense* involved holding up an ideal life to contrast with the present, one that would save us from the need to commit ourselves to the situation surrounding us. It was a pattern akin to that found in certain religions, in which life on earth is only a prelude to an ever-lasting and far more pleasant heavenly existence. Our attitude towards holidays, parties, work and perhaps love had something immortal to it, as though we would be on the earth for long enough not to stoop so low as to think these occasions finite in number – and hence be forced to draw value from them. There is comfort in living in the future perfect tense: it prevents one from needing to feel the present is real, or from realizing we must love one another or die.

9.   If Chloe had now fallen ill, was it not perhaps because the present was catching up with her dissatisfaction? It had, for a brief moment, ceased to lack anything the future might hold. But was I not just as guilty of the disease as Chloe? Had there

not been many times when the pleasures of the present had been rudely passed over in the name of an unnameable future, love stories in which, almost imperceptibly, I had abstained from loving fully, comforting myself with the immortal thought that there would be other love affairs I would one day try to enjoy with the insouciance of men in magazines, future loves that would redeem my calamitous efforts to communicate with another whom history had set spinning on the earth at much the same time?

10.   But longing for a future that never comes is only the flipside of longing for a time that is always past. Is not the past often better simply because it is past? I recalled that as a child every holiday grew perfect only when it was over, for then the anxiety of the present would have been reduced to a few containable memories. It did not matter so much what happened as that it all should happen as soon as possible, leaving me to nurse a wound or replay a joy. I spent whole childhood years looking forward to the winter holidays, when the family drove up from Zurich to spend two weeks skiing in the Engadine. But when I was finally on top of the slope, looking down a pristine white piste, I would be aware of an anxiety that would have evaporated from the memory of the event, a memory that was composed of only the objective conditions [the top of a mountain, a brilliant day] and would hence be free of everything that had made the actual moment hell. It was more than the fact I might have had a runny nose, or been thirsty, or forgotten a scarf that made the present unpleasant – it was a simple reluctance to accept that I was finally going to live out a possibility that had all year resided in the comforting

folds of the future. The skiing, sandwiched between mouth-watering anticipation and rosy memory, lost no time in sliding over the present. As soon as I had reached the bottom of the slope, I would look back up the mountain and declare to myself that it had been a perfect and wonderful run. And so the skiing holiday [and much of my life generally] would proceed: antici-pation in the morning, anxiety in the actuality, and pleasant memories in the evening.

11.   There was for a long time something of this tense paradox in my relationship with Chloe: I would spend all day looking forward to a meal with her, would come away from it with the best impressions, but find myself faced with a present that had never equalled its anticipation or memory. It was one evening shortly before we'd left for Spain, on Will Knott's houseboat with Chloe and other friends, when, because everything was so perfect, I first grew unavoidably aware of my lingering sus-picions towards the present moment. Most of the time, the present is too flawed to remind us that the disease of living in the *present imperfect tense* is within us, and nothing to do with the world outside. But that evening in Chelsea, there was simply nothing I could fault the moment on and hence had to realize that the problem lay within me: the food was delicious, friends were there, Chloe was looking beautiful, sitting next to me and holding my hand. And yet something was wrong all the same, the fact that I could not wait till the event had slipped into history.

12.   The inability to live in the present perhaps lies in the fear of realizing that this may be the arrival of what one has longed

for all of one's life, the fear of leaving the relatively sheltered position of anticipation or memory, and hence tacitly admitting that this is the only life that one is ever likely [heavenly intervention aside] to live. If commitment is seen as a group of eggs, then to commit oneself to the present is to risk putting all one's eggs in the present basket, rather than distributing them between the baskets of past and future. And to shift the analogy to love, to finally accept that I was happy with Chloe would have meant accepting that, despite the danger, all of my eggs were firmly in her basket.

13.   Whatever pills the good doctor had given her, Chloe seemed completely cured the next morning. We prepared a picnic and went back to the lake, where we passed the day swimming and reading by the water. We spent ten days in Spain, and I believe [as much as one can trust memory] that for the first time, we both risked living those days in the present. Living in this tense did not always mean bliss; the anxieties created by love's unstable happiness routinely exploded into argument. I remember a furious row in the village of Fuentelespino de Moya, where we had stopped for lunch. It had started as a joke about an old girlfriend, and had grown into a suspicion in Chloe's mind that I was still in love with her. Nothing could have been further from the truth, yet I had taken such suspicion to be a projection of Chloe's own declining feelings for me and accused her of as much. By the time the arguing, sulking and reconciliations were over, it was midafternoon, and we were both left wondering what the tears and shouts had been about. There were other arguments. I remember one near the village of Losa del Obispo about whether or not we were bored with

one another, another near Sot de Chera that had started after I had accused Chloe of being an incompetent map reader and she had countered the charge by accusing me of cartographic fascism.

14. The reasons for such arguments were never the surface ones: whatever Chloe's deficiencies with the *Guide Michelin*, or my intolerance to driving around in large circles through the Spanish countryside, what was at stake were far deeper anxieties. The strength of the accusations we made, their sheer implausibility, showed that we argued not because we hated one another, but because we loved one another too much – or, to risk confusing things, because we hated loving one another to the extent we did. Our accusations were loaded with a complicated subtext, *I hate you, because I love you*. It amounted to a fundamental protest, *I hate having no choice but to risk loving you like this*. The pleasures of depending on someone pale next to the paralysing fears that such dependence involves. Our occasionally fierce and somewhat inexplicable arguments during our trip through Valencia were nothing but a necessary release of tension that came from realizing that each one had placed all their eggs in the other's basket – and was helpless to aim for more sound household management. Our arguments sometimes had an almost theatrical quality to them, a joy and exuberance would manifest itself as we set about destroying the bookshelf, smashing the crockery or slamming doors: 'It's nice being able to feel I can hate you like this,' Chloe once said to me. 'It reassures me that you can take it, that I can tell you to fuck off and you'll throw something at me but stay put.' We needed to shout at one another partly to see whether or not we could

tolerate each other's shouting. We wanted to test each other's capacity for survival: only if we had tried in vain to destroy one another would we know we were safe.

15.   It is easiest to accept happiness when it is brought about through things that one can control, that one has achieved after much effort and reason. But the happiness I had reached with Chloe had not come after deep philosophizing or as a result of any personal achievement. It was simply the outcome of having, by a miracle of divine intervention, found a person whose company was more valuable to me than that of almost anyone in the world. Such happiness was dangerous precisely because it was so lacking in self-sufficient permanence. Had I after months of steady labour produced a scientific formula that had rocked the world of molecular biology, I would have had no qualms about accepting the happiness that had ensued from such a discovery. The difficulty of accepting the happiness Chloe represented came from my absence in the causal process leading to it, and hence my lack of control over the happiness-inducing element in my life. It seemed to have been arranged by the gods, and was hence accompanied by all the primitive fear of divine retribution.

16.   'All of man's unhappiness comes from an inability to stay in his room alone,' said Pascal, advocating a need for man to build up his own resources over and against a debilitating dependence on the social sphere. But how could this possibly be achieved in love? Proust tells the story of Mohammed II who, sensing that he was falling in love with one of the wives in the harem, at once had her killed because he did not wish to live

in spiritual bondage to another. Short of this, I had long ago given up hopes of achieving self-sufficiency. I had gone out of my room, and begun to love another – thereby taking on the risk inseparable from basing one's life around another human being.

17.   The anxiety of loving Chloe was in part the anxiety of being in a position where the cause of my happiness might so easily vanish, where she might suddenly lose interest, die, or marry another. At the height of love, there hence appeared a temptation to end the relationship prematurely, so that either Chloe or I could play at being the instigator of the end, rather than see the other partner, or habit, or familiarity end things. We were sometimes seized by an urge [manifested in our arguments about nothing] to kill our love affair before it had reached its natural end, a murder committed not out of hatred, but out of an excess of love – or rather, out of the fear that an excess of love may bring. Lovers may kill their own love story only because they are unable to tolerate the uncertainty, the sheer risk, that their experiment in happiness has delivered.

18.   Hanging over every love story is the thought, as horrible as it is unknowable, of how it will end. It is as when, in full health and vigour, we try to imagine our own death, the only difference between the end of love and the end of life being that at least in the latter, we are granted the comforting thought that we will not feel anything *after* death. No such comfort for the lover, who knows that the end of the relationship will not necessarily be the end of love, and almost certainly not the end of life.

CHAPTER SEVENTEEN

CONTRACTIONS

1. It was at first hard for me to imagine an untruth lasting 3.2 seconds fitted into a sequence of eight 0.8 second contractions, the first and the last two [3.2s] of which were genuine. It was easier to imagine a complete truth, or a complete lie, but the idea of a truth-lie-truth pattern seemed perverse and unnecessary. Either the whole sequence should have been false or the whole genuine. Perhaps I should have disregarded intentionality in favour of a physiological explanation. Yet whatever the cause and whatever the level of explanation, I had begun to notice that Chloe had [since our return from Spain] begun to simulate all or part of her orgasms.

$$0.8+/0.8+/0.8-/0.8-/0.8-/0.8-/0.8+/0.8+ = \textit{total length } 6.4\,[4]$$

2. Her usual number of contractions was replaced by an exaggerated activity, possibly designed to divert me from her lack of true involvement in the process. If I placed such interest in the appearance or non-appearance of contractions, it was not because contractions were *per se* important [there was evidence to show pleasure was not related to number], simply that they

---

[4] + = positive contraction, − = absence

were a significant symbol in a woman [who had in the past enjoyed a rapid number of contractions] of a possible wider trend towards disassociation.

3.　This declining number of contractions was not accompanied by any obvious sign of disinterest. In a sense, love making became all the more passionate at precisely this time. Not only was it performed more often, it was also performed in different positions and at different hours of the day, it was more turbulent, there were screams, even crying, the gestures almost crazed, closer to anger than the gentleness normally associated with the act. How much should have been read into this, I could not be certain. It suffices to mention that suspicion was aroused.

4.　What should have been said to Chloe was shared with a male friend instead.

'I don't know what's happening, Will, sex simply isn't what it used to be.'

'Don't worry, it goes in phases, you can't expect it to be high octane every time.'

'I don't. I just feel something else is wrong, I don't know what, but in the months since we came back from Spain, I've been noticing stuff. And I don't mean only in the bedroom, that's just a kind of symptom. I mean everywhere.'

'Like?'

'Well, nothing I could put a finger on directly. All right, here's one thing I remember. She likes a different cereal than me, but because I spend a lot of time at her place, she usually buys the kind of cereal I like so we can have breakfast together. Then all of a sudden last week, she stops buying it, and says it's too expensive. I don't want to come to any conclusions, I'm just noticing.'

5.   Will and I were standing in the reception area of our office. A cocktail party was in progress to celebrate the firm's twentieth birthday. I had brought Chloe with me, for whom this was a first chance to see my work-space.

'Why does Will have so many more commissions than you?' Chloe asked Will and me after wandering around the exhibits.

'You answer that one, Will.'

'That's because real geniuses always have a hard time getting their work accepted,' answered Will charitably.

'Your designs are brilliant,' Chloe told him, 'I've never seen anything so inventive, especially for office projects. The use of materials is just incredible, and the way you've managed to integrate the brick and metal so well. Couldn't you do things like that?' Chloe asked me.

'I'm working on a number of ideas, but my style is very different, I work with different materials.'

'Well, I think Will's work is great, incredible in fact. I'm so glad I came to see it.'

'Chloe, it's great to hear you say so,' answered Will.

'I'm so impressed, your work is exactly the kind of thing I'm interested in and I think it's such a pity that more architects don't do what you're trying to do. I imagine it can't be easy.'

'It's not that easy, but I've always been taught to go with

179

the things I believe in. I build the houses that make me feel real, and then the people who live in them end up absorbing a kind of energy from them.'

'I think I see what you mean.'

'You'd see better if we were out in California. I was working on a project in Monterey, and I mean, there you'd really get a sense of what you can do by using different kinds of stone as well as some steel and aluminium, and working *with* the landscape instead of *against* it.'

6.   It is part of good manners not to question the criteria responsible for eliciting another's love. The dream is that one has not been loved for criteria at all, but rather *for who one is*, an ontological status beyond properties or attributes. From within love, as within wealth, a taboo surrounds the means of acquiring and sustaining affection/property. Only poverty, either of love or money, leads one to question the system – perhaps the reason why lovers do not make great revolutionaries.

7.   Passing an unfortunate woman in the street one day, Chloe had asked me, 'Would you have loved me if I'd had an enormous birth mark on my face like her?' The yearning is that the answer be 'yes' – an answer that would place love above the mundane surfaces of the body, or more particularly, its cruel unchangeable ones. I will love you not just for your wit and talent and beauty, but simply because you are you, with no strings attached. I love you for who you are deep in your soul, not for the colour of your eyes or the length of your legs or size of your chequebook. The longing is that the lover admire us stripped of our external assets, appreciating the essence of our

being without accomplishments, ready to repeat the uncondi-
tional love said to exist in some parts between parent and child.
The real self is what one can freely choose to be, and if a
birthmark arises on our forehead or age withers us or recession
bankrupts us, then we must be excused for accidents that have
damaged what is only our surface. And even if we are beautiful
and rich, then we do not wish to be loved on account of these
things, for they may fail us, and with them, love. I would prefer
you to compliment me on my brain than on my face, but if you
must, then I would rather you comment on my smile [motor
and muscle controlled] than on my nose [static and tissue
based]. The desire is that I be loved even if I lost everything:
leaving nothing but 'me', this mysterious 'me' taken to be the
self at its weakest, most vulnerable point. *Do you love me enough
that I may be weak with you?* Everyone loves strength, but *Do you
love me for my weakness?* That is the real test. Do you love me
stripped of everything that might be lost, for only the things I
will have for ever?

8.   That evening at the architectural office, I first began to
sense Chloe slipping away from me, losing admiration for my
work and beginning to question my value in relation to other
men. Because I was tired, and Chloe and Will were not, I went
home and they chose to go on to the West End for a drink.
Chloe told me she'd call as soon as she got home, but by eleven
o'clock, I decided to call her. The answerphone replied, as it did
when I called again at two thirty that morning. The urge was to
confess my anxieties into the machine, but to formulate them
seemed to bring them closer into existence, dragging a suspicion
into the realm of accusation and counter-accusation. Perhaps it

was nothing – or at least everything: I preferred to imagine her in an accident than playing truant with Will. I called the police at four in the morning, and asked them in the most responsible tone a man drunk on vodka may adopt, if they had not seen evidence, perhaps a mutilated body or wrecked Volkswagen, of my angel in a short green skirt and black jacket, last seen in an office near the Barbican. No, sir, no such sighting had been made, was she a relative or just a friend? Could I wait till morning, and contact the station again then?

9. *'One can think problems into existence,'* Chloe had told me. I dared not think, for fear of what I might find. The freedom to think is the courage to stumble upon our demons. But the frightened mind cannot wander, I stayed tethered to my para-noia, brittle as glass. Bishop Berkeley and later Chloe had said that if one shuts one's eyes, the outer world may be said to be no more real than a dream, and now more than ever, the power of illusion came to seem comforting, the urge not to look truth in the face, the urge that if only one did not think, an unpleasant truth might not exist.

10. Feeling implicated in her absence, guilty for my sus-picions, and angry at my own guilt, I pretended to have noticed nothing when Chloe and I met at ten o'clock the following day. Yet she must have been guilty – for why else would she have gone to her local supermarket to add to her kitchen the missing breakfast cereal to fill Young Werther's stomach? She accused herself not by her indifference, but by her sense of duty, a large packet of Three Cereal Golden Bran prominently placed on the window ledge.

'Is something wrong with it? Isn't that the one you like?' asked Chloe, watching me stumble over my mouthfuls.

11.   She said she had stayed the night at her girlfriend Paula's house. Will and she had chatted till late in a bar in Soho, and as she'd had a bit to drink, it had seemed easier to stop off in Bloomsbury than make the journey back home to Islington. She had wanted to call me, but it would surely have woken me up. I had said I wanted to go to sleep early, so wasn't it the best thing? Why was I making that face? Did I want more milk to go with the three cereals?

12.   An urge accompanies epistemically stunted accounts of reality – the urge, if they are pleasant, to believe them. Like an optimistic simpleton's view of the world, Chloe's version of her evening was desirably believable, like a hot bath in which I wished to sit for ever. *If she believes in it, why shouldn't I? If it's this simple for her, why should it be so complicated for me?* I wished to be taken in by her story of a night spent on the floor of Paula's flat in Bloomsbury, able in that case to set aside my alternative evening [another bed, another man, contractions]. Like the voter from whom the politician's caramel promise draws a tear, I was lured by falsehood's ability to appeal to my deepest emotional yearning.

13.   Therefore, as she had spent the night with Paula, had bought cereal and all was forgiven, I felt a burst of confidence and relief, like a man awaking from a nightmare. I got up from the table and put my arms around the beloved's thick white pullover, caressing her shoulders through the wool, then bend-

ing down to kiss her neck, nibbling at her ear, feeling the familiar perfume of her skin and the brush of her hair against my face. *'Don't, not now,'* said the angel. But, disbelieving, caught up in the familiar perfume of her skin and brush of hair against his face, Cupid continued to pucker his lips against her flesh. *'I said once already, not now!'* repeated the angel, so that even he might hear.

14.   The pattern of the kiss had been formed during their first night together. She had placed her head beside his and, fascinated by this soft juncture between mind and body, he had begun running his lips along the curve of her neck. It had made her shudder and smile, she had played with his hand, and shut her eyes. It had become a routine between them, a signature of their intimate language. *Don't, not now.* Hate is the hidden script in the letter of love, its foundations are shared with its opposite. The woman seduced by her partner's way of kissing her neck, turning the pages of a book or telling a joke watches irritation collect at precisely these junctures. It is as if the end of love was already contained in its beginning, the ingredients of love's collapse eerily foreshadowed by those of its creation.

15.   *I said once already, not now.* There are cases of skilled doctors, experts at detecting the first signs of cancer in their patients, who will somehow ignore the growth of football-sized tumours in their own body. There are examples of people who in most walks of life are clear and rational, but who are unable to accept that one of their children has died or that their wife or husband has left them – and will continue to believe the child has merely gone missing or the spouse will leave their new

marriage for the old. The shipwrecked lover cannot accept the evidence of the wreckage, continuing to behave as though nothing had changed, in the vain hope that by ignoring the verdict of execution, death will somehow be stalled. The signs of death were everywhere waiting to be read – had I not been struck by the illiteracy pain had induced.

16.   The victim of love's demise grows unable to locate original strategies to revive the corpse. At precisely the time when things might still have been rescued with ingenuity, fearful *and hence unoriginal*, I became nostalgic. Sensing Chloe drawing away, I attempted to pull her back through blind repetition of elements that had in the past cemented us. I continued with the kiss, and in the weeks thereafter, insisted that we return to cinemas and restaurants where we had spent pleasant evenings, I revisited jokes we had laughed at together, I readopted positions our bodies had once moulded.

17.   I sought comfort in the familiarity of our in-house language, the language used to ease previous conflicts, the Heraclitean joke designed to acknowledge and hence render inoffensive the temporary fluctuations of love.

'Is something wrong today?' I asked one morning when Venus looked almost as pale and sad as I.

'Today?'

'Yes, today, is something wrong?'

'No, why? Is there any reason it should be?'

'I don't think so.'

'So why are you asking?'

'I don't know. Because you're looking a bit unhappy.'

'Sorry for being human.'

'I'm just trying to help. Out of ten today, what would you give me?'

'I really don't know.'

'Why not?'

'I'm tired.'

'Just tell me.'

'I can't.'

'Come on, out of ten. Six? Three? Minus twelve? Plus twenty?'

'I don't know.'

'Have a guess.'

'For Christ's sake, I don't know, leave me alone, damn it!'

18.   The in-house language unravelled, it grew unfamiliar to Chloe, or rather, she feigned forgetting, so as not to admit denial. She refused complicity in the language, she played the foreigner, she began reading me against the grain, and found errors. I could not understand why things I was saying and that in the past had proved so attractive were now suddenly so irritating. I could not understand why, having not changed myself, I should now be accused of being offensive in a hundred different ways. Panicking, I embarked on an attempt to return to the golden age, asking myself, '*What had I been doing then that I perhaps am not doing now?*' I became a desperate conformist to a past self that had been the object of love. What I had failed to realize was that the past self was the one now proving so annoying, and that I was therefore doing nothing but accelerating the process towards dissolution.

19.   I became an irritant, *one who has gone beyond caring for reciprocation*. I bought her books, I took her jackets to the dry cleaner's, I paid for dinner, I suggested we make a trip to Paris at Christmas time to celebrate our anniversary. But humiliation could be the only result of loving against all evidence. She could sulk me, shout at me, ignore me, tease me, trick me, hit me, kick me, and still I would not react – and thereby grew abhorrent.

20.   At the end of a meal I had spent two hours preparing [largely taken up by an argument over Balkan history], I took Chloe's hand and told her, 'I just wanted to say, and I know it sounds sentimental, that however much we fight and everything, I still really care about you and want things to work out between us. You mean everything to me, you know that.'

Chloe [who had always read more psychoanalysis than novels] looked at me suspiciously and replied, 'Listen, it's kind of you to say so, but it worries me; you've got to stop turning me into your ego ideal like this.'

21.   Things had reduced themselves to a tragi-comic scenario: on the one hand, the man identifying the woman as an angel, on the other, the angel identifying love as something short of a pathology.

CHAPTER EIGHTEEN

ROMANTIC TERRORISM

1.   *Why don't you love me?* is as impossible a question [though a far less pleasant one], to ask as *Why do you love me?* In both cases, we come up against our lack of conscious [seductive] control in the amorous structure, the fact that love has been brought to us as a gift for reasons we never wholly determine or *deserve*. In a sense, the answer is not for us to know, it can explain nothing because we cannot act on its revelations. It is not a causally effective reason, it comes after the fact, a justification for more subterranean shifts, a superficial *post hoc* analysis. To ask such questions, we are forced to veer on one side towards complete arrogance, on the other to complete humility: *What have I done to deserve love?* asks the humble lover; I can have done nothing. *What have I done to be denied love?* protests the betrayed one, arrogantly claiming possession of a gift that is never one's due. To both questions, the one who hands out love can only reply *Because you are you* – an answer that swings the beloved dangerously and unpredictably between grandiosity and depression.

2.   Love may be born at first sight, but it does not die with corresponding rapidity. Chloe must have feared that to talk or even leave would have been hasty, that she might have been

opting for a life offering no more favourable alternative. It was hence a slow separation, the masonry of affect only gradually prising itself loose from the loved one's body. There was guilt at the infidelity implied, guilt at the residual sense of responsibility towards a once prized object, a form of treacly liquid left at the bottom of the glass that needed time to drain off.

3.   When every decision is difficult, no decision is taken. Chloe prevaricated, I joined her [for how could any decision be pleasant for me?]. We continued to see one another and sleep with one another and made plans to visit Paris at Christmas time. Yet Chloe was curiously disengaged from the process, as though she were making plans for someone else – perhaps because it was easier to deal in airline tickets than the issues that lay behind their purchase or non-purchase. Her lack of decision embodied the hope that by doing nothing, another might take the decision for her, that by displaying her indecision and frustration while not acting on it, I would ultimately perform the move that she had needed [but been too scared] to make herself.

4.   We entered the age of romantic terrorism.
      'Is there anything wrong?'
      'No, why, should there be?'
      'I just thought you might want to talk about things.'
      'What things?'
      'About us.'
      'You mean about you,' snapped Chloe.
      'No, I mean about us.'
      'Well what about us?'

'I don't know, really. It's just a sense I have that ever since about the middle of September, we haven't really been communicating. It's like there's a wall between us and you're refusing to acknowledge it's there.'

'I don't see a wall.'

'That's what I mean. You're even refusing to admit there was ever anything other than this.'

'Than what?'

5.   Once a partner has begun to lose interest, there is apparently little the other can do to arrest the process. Like seduction, withdrawal suffers under a blanket of reticence, an unmentionable issue at the centre of the relationship: *I desire you/I don't desire you* – in both cases, it takes an age for either message to find articulation. The very breakdown of communication is hard to discuss, unless both parties have a desire to see it restored. This leaves the lover in a desperate situation: the charms and seduction of legitimate dialogue seem exhausted and produce only irritation. In so far as the lover acts legitimately [sweetly], it is normally *ironic* action, action that smothers love in the attempt to revive it. And so at this point, desperate to woo the partner back at any cost, the lover turns to romantic terrorism, the product of irredeemable situations, a gamut of tricks [sulking, jealousy, guilt] that attempt to force the partner to return love, by blowing up [in fits of tears, rage or otherwise] in front of the loved one. The terroristic partner knows he or she cannot realistically hope to see their love reciprocated, but the futility of something is not always [in love or in politics] a sufficient argument against it. Certain things are said not because they will be heard, but because it is important to speak.

6.   When political dialogue has failed to resolve a grievance, the injured party may in desperation resort to terrorist activity, extracting by force the concession it has been unable to seduce peacefully from its opposite number. Political terrorism is born out of deadlocked situations, behaviour that combines a party's need to act with an awareness [conscious or semi-conscious] that action will not go any way towards achieving the desired end – and will if anything only alienate the other party further. The negativity of terrorism betrays all the signs of childish rage, a rage at one's own impotence in the face of a more powerful adversary.

7.   In May 1972, three members of the Japanese Red Army, who had been armed, briefed and financed by the Popular Front for the Liberation of Palestine [PFLP], landed on a regular scheduled flight at Lod Airport, near Tel Aviv. They disembarked, followed the other passengers into the terminal building and once inside, pulled machine-guns and grenades out of their hand luggage. They began firing on the crowd indiscriminately, slaughtering twenty-four people and injuring a further seven, before they were themselves killed by the security forces. What relation did such butchery have with the cause of Palestinian autonomy? The murders did not accelerate the peace process, they only hardened Israeli public opinion against the Palestinian cause, and in a final irony for the terrorists, it turned out the majority of their victims were not even Israelis, but belonged to a party of Puerto Rican Christians who had been on a religious pilgrimage to Jerusalem. Yet the action found its justification elsewhere, in the need to vent frustration in a cause where dialogue had ceased to produce results.

8.   Both of us could only spare a weekend in Paris, so we left on the last flight out of Heathrow on Friday, and planned to return late on the Sunday. Though we were going to France to celebrate our anniversary, it felt more like a funeral. When the plane landed in Paris, the airport terminal was sombre and empty. It had begun to snow and a fierce arctic wind was blowing. There were more passengers than taxis, so we ended up sharing a ride with a woman we had met at passport control, a lawyer travelling from London to Paris for a conference. Though the woman was attractive, I was in no mood to find her so, but nevertheless flirted with her as we made our way into the city. When Chloe attempted to join the conversation, I would interrupt her with a remark addressed exclusively [and seductively] to the woman. But success in inducing jealousy is dependent on a significant factor: the inclination of the targeted audience to give a damn. Hence terroristic jealousy is always a gamble: how far could I go in trying to make Chloe jealous? What if she were not to react? Whether she was merely hiding that jealousy so as to call my bluff [like politicians who appear on television and declare how unconcerned they are with the terrorist threat], or whether she genuinely did not care, I could not be sure. But one thing was certain, Chloe did not allow me the pleasure of a jealous reaction, and was more pleasant than she had been in a long time when we finally settled into our room in a small hotel on the Rue Jacob.

9.   Terrorists take a gamble in assuming their actions will prove terrifying enough to provide a form of bargaining power. There is the story of a wealthy Italian businessman who late one afternoon received a phone call in his office from a terrorist

gang, telling him they had kidnapped his youngest daughter. A huge sum was stipulated as ransom, and a threat was made that if the ransom was not paid, the father would never see his daughter alive again. But the businessman did not panic and casually replied that if they killed his daughter, they would in fact be doing him an enormous favour. He explained that he had ten children, and that they had all been a disappointment and a trial to him, expensive to keep and the unfortunate result of only a few moments of exertion in the bedroom on his part. The ransom would not be paid, and if they wanted to kill her, that was their choice. And with that blunt message, the businessman put down the phone. The terrorist group believed him, and within hours, the girl was released.

10.   It was still snowing when we awoke the next morning, but it was too warm for it to settle, so the pavements turned to mud, brown beneath a low grey sky. We had decided to visit the Musée d'Orsay after breakfast, and planned to go on to a cinema in the afternoon. I had just shut the door to the hotel room, when Chloe asked me brusquely, 'Have you got the key?'

'No,' I answered, 'you told me a minute ago you had it.'

'Did I? No I didn't,' said Chloe, 'I don't have the key. You've just locked us out.'

'I haven't locked us out. I shut the door thinking you had the key, because the key wasn't where I left it.'

'Well, that's really silly of you, because I don't have it either, so we're locked out – thanks to *you*.'

'Thanks to me! For Heaven's sake, stop blaming me for the fact that it was you who forgot the key.'

'I had nothing to do with the key.'

At that moment, Chloe turned towards the lifts, and [with novelistic timing] the room key fell out of her coat pocket on to the maroon carpet of the hotel.

'Oh, I'm sorry. I did have it all along, oh, well,' said Chloe.

But I decided I would not forgive her with ease, and snapped, 'That's it,' and headed for the stairs silently and melodramatically, Chloe calling after me, 'Wait, don't be silly, where are you going? I said I was sorry.'

11.   A structurally successful terroristic sulk must be sparked by some wrong-doing, however small, on the part of the sulked, and yet is marked by a disproportion between insult inflicted and sulk elicited, drawing a punishment bearing little relation to the severity of the original offence – and one that cannot easily be resolved through normal channels. I had been waiting to sulk Chloe for a long time, but to begin sulking when one has not been wronged in any definite way is counter-productive, for there is a danger the partner will not notice and guilt not flourish.

12.   I could briefly have shouted at Chloe, she back at me, and then our argument over the room key would have unwound itself. At the basis of all sulks lies a wrong that might have been addressed and disappeared at once, but that instead is taken by the injured partner and stored for later and more painful detonation. Delays in explanations give grievances a weight that they would lack if the matter had been addressed as soon as it had arisen. To display anger shortly after an offence occurs is the most generous thing one may do, for it saves the sulked

from the burgeoning of guilt and the need to talk the sulker down from his or her battlement. I did not wish to do Chloe such a favour, so I walked out of the hotel alone and headed towards Saint Germain, where I spent two hours browsing in a series of bookshops. Then, instead of returning to the hotel to leave a message, I ate lunch alone in a restaurant, then went to see two films in a row, eventually returning to the hotel at seven o'clock in the evening.

13.   The key point about terrorism is that it is primarily designed to attract attention, a form of psychological warfare with goals [for instance, the creation of a Palestinian state] unrelated to military techniques [opening fire in the arrival lounge of Lod Airport]. There is a discrepancy between means and ends, a sulk being used to make a point relatively unconnected to the sulk itself – *I am angry at you for accusing me of losing the key* symbolizing the wider [but unspeakable] message *I am angry at you for no longer loving me*.

14.   Chloe was no brute and, whatever I might claim, had generous tendencies for self-blame. She had tried to follow me to Saint Germain, but had lost me in the crowd. She had returned to the hotel, waited a while, and then gone to the Musée d'Orsay. When I finally came back to the room, I found her resting in bed, but without speaking to her, went into the bathroom and took a long shower.

15.   The sulker is a complicated creature, giving off messages of deep ambivalence, crying out for help and attention, while at the same time rejecting it should it be offered, *wanting to be*

understood without needing to speak. Chloe asked if she could be forgiven, saying she hated to leave arguments unresolved and wanted us to spend a pleasant anniversary evening that night. I said nothing. Unable to express the full extent of my anger with her [an anger that had nothing to do with a key], I had grown unreasonable. Why had it become so hard for me to say what I meant? Because of the danger of communicating my real grievance; that Chloe had ceased to love me. My hurt was so inexpressible, had so little to do with a forgotten key that I would have looked like a fool to bring the matter up at this stage. My anger was hence forced underground. Unable to say directly what I meant, I had resorted to symbolizing meaning, half hoping, half dreading that the symbol would be decoded.

16.   After my shower, we finally made it up over the key incident, and went out for dinner to a restaurant on the Île de la Cité. We were both on best behaviour, keen to avoid tensions, chatting on neutral territory about books, films, and capital cities. It might have seemed [from the waiter's point of view] that the couple was indeed a happy one – and that romantic terrorism had scored a significant victory.

17.   Yet ordinary terrorists have a distinct advantage over romantic terrorists, the fact that their demands [however out-rageous] do not include the most outrageous demand of all, the demand *to be loved*. I knew that the happiness we were enjoying that evening in Paris was illusory, because the love that Chloe was displaying had not been given spontaneously. It was the love of a woman who feels guilty for the fact she has ceased to feel affection, but who nevertheless attempts a display of loyalty

196

[as much to convince herself as her partner]. Hence my evening was not a happy one: my sulk had worked, but its success had been empty.

18.   Though ordinary terrorists may occasionally force concessions from governments by blowing up buildings or school children, romantic terrorists are doomed to disappointment because of a fundamental inconsistency in their approach. *You must love me*, says the romantic terrorist, *I will force you to love me by sulking you or making you feel jealous*, but then comes the paradox, for if love is returned, it is at once considered tainted, and the romantic terrorist must complain, *If I have only forced you to love me, then I cannot accept this love, for it was not spontaneously given*. Romantic terrorism is a demand that negates itself in the process of its resolution, it brings the terrorist up against an uncomfortable reality – that love's death cannot be arrested.

19.   As we walked back towards the hotel, Chloe slipped her hand in my coat pocket and kissed me on the cheek. I did not return her kiss, not because a kiss was not the most desired conclusion to a terrible day, simply because I could no longer feel Chloe's kiss to be genuine. I had lost the will to force love on its unwilling recipient.

CHAPTER NINETEEN

BEYOND GOOD AND EVIL

1.   Early on Sunday evening, Chloe and I were sitting in the economy section of a British Airways jet, making our way back from Paris to London. We had recently crossed the Normandy coast, where a blanket of winter cloud had given way to an uninterrupted view of dark waters below. Tense and unable to concentrate, I shifted uncomfortably in my seat. There was something threatening about the flight, the dull background throb of the engines, the hushed grey interior, the candy smiles of the airline employees. A trolley carrying a selection of drinks and snacks was making its way down the aisle and, though I was both hungry and thirsty, it filled me with the vague nausea that meals may elicit in aircraft.

2.   Chloe had been listening to her Walkman while dozing, but she now pulled out the plugs from her ears and stared with her large watery eyes at the seat in front of her.

'Are you all right?' I asked.

There was a silence, as though she had not heard. Then she spoke.

'You're too good for me,' she said.

'What?'

'I said, "You're too good for me."'

'What? Why?'

'Because you are.'

'What are you saying this for, Chloe?'

'I don't know.'

'If anything, I'd put it the other way round. You're always the one ready to make the effort when there's a problem, you're just more self-deprecating about your . . .'

'Shush, stop, don't,' said Chloe, turning her head away from me.

'Why?'

'Because I've been seeing Will.'

'*You've what?*'

'I've been seeing Will, OK.'

'What? What does *seeing* mean? *Seeing* Will?'

'For God's sake, I've been to bed with Will.'

'Would madam like a beverage or light snack?' enquired the stewardess, arriving with her trolley at that moment.

'No, thank you.'

'Nothing at all, then?'

'No, I'm all right.'

'How about for sir?'

'No thanks, nothing.'

3.   Chloe had started to cry.

'I can't believe this. I just cannot believe this. Tell me it's a joke, some terrible, horrible joke, you've been to bed with Will. When? How? How could you?'

'God, I'm so sorry, I really am. I'm sorry, but I . . . I . . . I'm sorry . . .'

Chloe was crying so hard, she was unable to speak. Tears

were streaming down her face, her nose was running, her whole body shaken by spasms, her breathing halting, gasping. She looked in such pain, for a moment I forgot the import of her revelation, concerned only to stop the flow of her tears.

'Chloe, please don't cry, it's all right. We can talk about this. Tidge, please, take this handkerchief. It'll be OK, it will, I promise . . .'

'My God, I'm so sorry, God I'm sorry, you don't deserve this, you really don't.'

Chloe's devastation temporarily eased the burden of betrayal. Her tears represented a brief reprieve for my own. The irony of the situation was not lost on me – the lover comforting his beloved for the upset betraying him has caused her.

4.　The tears might have drowned every last passenger and sunk the whole aeroplane had the captain not prepared to land soon after they had begun. It felt like the Flood, a deluge of sadness on both sides at the inevitability and cruelty of what was happening: it simply wasn't working, it was going to have to end. Things felt all the more lonely, all the more exposed in our material surroundings, the technological environment of the cabin, the clinical attentions of stewardesses, fellow passengers staring with the smug relief others feel in the face of strangers' emotional crises.

5.　As the plane pierced through the clouds, I tried to imagine a future: a period of life was coming brutally to an end, and I had nothing to replace it with, only a terrifying absence. *We hope you enjoy your stay in London, and will choose to fly with us again soon*. To fly again soon, but would I live again soon? I envied the assumptions of others, the security of fixed lives and plans to take-off again soon. What would life mean from now on? Though we continued holding hands, I knew how Chloe and I would watch our bodies grow foreign. Walls would be built up, the separation would be institutionalized, I would meet her in a few months or years, we would be light, jovial, masked, dressed for business, ordering a salad in a restaurant – unable to touch what only now we could reveal, the sheer human drama, the nakedness, the dependency, the unalterable loss. We would be like an audience emerging from a heart-wrenching play but unable to communicate anything of the emotions they had felt inside, able only to head for a drink at the bar, knowing there was more, but unable to touch it. Though it was agony, I preferred this moment to the ones that would come, the hours spent alone replaying it, blaming myself and her, trying to construct a future, an alternative story, like a confused playwright who does not know what to do with his characters [save kill them off for a neat ending . . .]. All this till the wheels hit the tarmac at Heathrow, the engines were thrown into reverse thrust, and the plane taxied towards the terminal, where it disgorged its cargo into the immigration hall. By the time Chloe and I had collected our luggage and passed through customs, the relationship was formally over. We would try to be good friends, we would try not to cry, we would try not to feel victims or executioners.

6.   Two days passed, numb. To suffer a blow and feel nothing – in modern parlance, it means the blow must have been hard

indeed. Then one morning, I received a hand-delivered letter from Chloe, her familiar black writing poured over two sheets of cream white paper:

> *I am sorry for offering you my confusion, I am sorry for ruining our trip to Paris, I am sorry for the unavoidable melodrama of it. I don't think I will ever cry again as much as I did aboard that miserable airplane, or be so torn by my emotions. You were so sweet to me, that's what made me cry all the more, other men would have told me to go to hell, but you didn't, and that's what made it so very difficult.*
>
> *You asked me in the terminal how I could cry and yet still be sure. You must understand, I cried because I knew it could not go on, and yet there was still so much holding me to you. I realize I cannot continue to deny you the love you deserve, but that I have grown unable to give you. It would be unfair, it would destroy us both.*
>
> *I shall never be able to write the letter which I would really want to write to you. This is not the letter I have been writing to you in my head for the last few days. I wish I could draw you a picture, I was never too good with a pen. I can't seem to say what I want, I only hope you'll fill in the blanks.*
>
> *I will miss you, nothing can take away what we have shared. I have loved the months we have spent together. It seems such a surreal combination of things, breakfasts, lunches, phone calls in mid-afternoon, late nights at the Electric, walks in Kensington Gardens. I don't want anything to spoil that. When you've been in love, it is not the length of time that matters, it's everything you've felt and done coming*

out intensified. To me, it's one of the few times when life isn't elsewhere. You'll always be beautiful to me, I'll never forget how much I adored waking up and finding you beside me. I simply don't wish to continue hurting you. I could not bear for it slowly all to go stale.

I don't know where I will go from here. I will perhaps spend time on my own over Christmas or spend it with my parents. Will is going to California soon, so we'll see. Don't be unfair, don't blame him. He likes you very much and respects you immensely. He was only a symptom, not the cause of what's happened. Excuse this messy letter, its confusion will probably be a reminder of the way I was with you. Forgive me, you were too good for me. I hope we can stay friends. All my love . . .

7.　The letter brought no relief, only reminders. I recognized the cadences and accent of her speech, carrying with it the image of her face, the smell of her skin – and the wound I had sustained. I wept at the finality of the letter, the situation confirmed, analysed, turned into the past tense. I could feel the doubts and ambivalence in her syntax, but the message was definitive. It was over, she was sorry it was over, but love had ebbed. I was overwhelmed by a sense of betrayal, betrayal because a relationship in which I had invested so much had been declared bankrupt without my feeling it to be so. Chloe had not given it a chance, I argued with myself, knowing the hopelessness of these inner courts announcing hollow verdicts at four thirty in the morning. Though there had been no contract, only the contract of the heart, I felt stung by Chloe's disloyalty, by her heresy, by her night with another man. How was it morally possible this should have been allowed to happen?

8.   It is surprising how often rejection in love is framed in moral language, the language of right and wrong, good and evil, as though to reject or not reject, to love or not to love, was something that naturally belonged to a branch of ethics. It is surprising how often the one who rejects is labelled evil, and the one who is rejected comes to embody the good. There was something of this moral attitude in both Chloe and my behaviour. Framing her rejection, she had equated her inability to love with evil, and my love for her as evidence of goodness – hence the conclusion, made on the basis of nothing more than that I still desired her, that I was 'too good' for her. Assuming that she largely meant what she said and was not simply being polite, she had made the ethical point that she was not good enough for me, by virtue of nothing more than having ceased to love me – something she had deemed made her a less worthy person than I, a man who, in all the goodness of his heart, still felt able to love her.

9.   But however unfortunate rejection may be, can we really equate loving with selflessness, and rejection with cruelty, can we really equate love with goodness and indifference with evil? Was my love for Chloe moral, and her rejection of me immoral? The guilt owed to Chloe for rejecting me depended primarily on the extent to which love could be seen as something that I had given selflessly – for if selfish motives entered into my gift, then Chloe was surely justified in equally selfishly ending the

relationship. Viewed from such a perspective, the end of love appeared to be a clash between two fundamentally selfish impulses, rather than between altruism and egoism, morality and immorality.

10.   According to Immanuel Kant, a moral action is to be distinguished from an immoral one by the fact that it is performed out of duty and regardless of the pain or pleasure involved. I am behaving morally only when I do something without consideration of what I may get in return for it, when I am guided solely by duty: 'For any action to be morally good, it is not enough that it should conform to the moral law – it must also be done for the sake of the moral law.'[5] Actions performed as a result of disposition cannot count as moral, a direct rejection of the utilitarian view of morality based around inclination. The essence of Kant's theory is that morality is to be found exclusively in the *motive* from which an act is performed. To love someone is moral only when that love is given free of any expected return, if that love is given simply for the sake of giving love.

11.   I called Chloe immoral because she had rejected the attentions of someone who had on a daily basis brought her comfort, encouragement, support and affection. But was she to blame in a *moral* sense for spurning these? Blame is surely due when we spurn a gift given at much cost and sacrifice, but if the giver has derived as much pleasure from giving as we derive

[5] *Groundwork of the Metaphysic of Morals*, Immanuel Kant, Harper Torch-books, 1964

from receiving, then is there really a case for using moral language? If love is primarily given out of selfish motivations [i.e. for one's own benefit even as it arises out of the benefit of the other], then it is not, in Kantian eyes at least, a moral gift. Was I better than Chloe simply because I loved her? Of course not, for though my love for her included sacrifices, I had made them because it made me happy to do so, I had not martyred myself, I had acted only because it accorded so perfectly with my inclinations, because it was *not* a duty.

12.   We spend our time loving like utilitarians, in the bedroom we are followers of Hobbes and Bentham, not Plato and Kant. We make moral judgements on the basis of preference, not transcendental values: as Hobbes had put it in his *Elements of Law*,

> 'Every man calleth that which pleaseth and is delightful to him, *good*; and that *evil* which displeaseth him: insomuch that while every man differeth from other in constitution, they differ also one from another concerning the common distinction of good and evil. Nor is there such thing as *agathon haplos*, that is to say, simply good . . .'[6]

13.   I had called Chloe evil because she 'displeaseth-ed' *me*, not because she was in herself inherently evil. My value system was a *justification* of a situation rather than an explanation of Chloe's offence according to an absolute standard. I had made the classic moralist's error, traced so succinctly by Nietzsche:

[6] *Elements of Law*, Thomas Hobbes, edt. Molesworth, 1839–45

'First of all, one calls individual actions good or bad quite irrespective of their motives but solely on account of their useful or harmful consequences. Soon, however, one forgets the origin of these designations and believes that the quality *good* and *evil* is inherent in the actions themselves, irrespective of their consequences. . .'[7]

What gave me pleasure and pain determined the moral labels I chose to affix to Chloe – I was an egocentric moralizer, judging the world and her duties within it according to my own interests. My moral code was a mere sublimation of my desires, a Platonic offence if ever there was one.

14.   At the summit of self-righteous despair, I asked, *'Is it not my right to be loved and her duty to love me?'* Chloe's love was indispensable, her presence in the bed beside me as important as freedom or the right to life. If the government assured me these two, why could it not assure me the right to love? Why did it place such an emphasis on the right to life and free speech when I didn't give a damn about either, without someone to lend that life meaning? What use was it to live if it was without love and without being heard? What was freedom if it meant the freedom to be abandoned?

15.   But how could one possibly extend the language of rights to love, to force people to love out of duty? Was this not simply another manifestation of romantic terrorism, of romantic fascism? Morality must have its boundaries. It is the stuff of High

[7] *Human, all too Human*, Friedrich Nietzsche, University of Nebraska Press, 1986

Courts, not of salty midnight tears and the heart-wrenching separations of well-fed, well-housed, over-read, over-cooked sentimentalists. I had only ever loved selfishly, spontaneously, like a utilitarian. And if utilitarianism states an action is right only when it produces the greatest happiness for the greatest number, then the pain now involved both in loving Chloe and hers in being loved was the surest sign that our relationship had not simply grown amoral, but immoral.

16.   It was unfortunate that anger could not be wedded to blame. Pain mobilized me to seek an offender, but responsibility could not be pinned on Chloe. I learnt that humans stood in a relation of negative liberty towards one another, dutybound not to hurt others, but certainly not forced to love one another if they did not wish. A primitive, non-tragic belief made me feel that my anger entitled me to blame another, but I recognized that blame could only be linked to choice. One does not get angry with a donkey for not being able to sing, for the donkey's constitution never gave it a chance to do anything but snort. Similarly, one cannot blame a lover for loving or not loving, for it is a matter beyond their choice and hence responsibility – though what makes rejection in love harder to bear than donkeys who can never sing is that one did once see the lover loving. One finds it easier not to blame the donkey for not singing because it never sang, but the lover loved, perhaps only a short while ago, which makes the reality of the claim *I cannot love you any more* all the harder to digest.

17.   The arrogance of wanting to be loved had emerged only now it was unreciprocated – I was left alone with my desire,

defenceless, right-less, beyond the law, shockingly crude in my demands: *Love me!* And for what reason? I had only the usual paltry excuse: *Because I love you* . . .

CHAPTER TWENTY

PSYCHO-FATALISM

1.   Whenever something calamitous happens to us, we are led
to look beyond everyday causal explanations in order to understand why we have been singled out to receive such terrible,
intolerable punishment. And the more devastating the event,
the more inclined we are to imbue it with a significance it does
not objectively have, the more likely we are to slip into a brand
of psycho-fatalism. Bewildered and exhausted by grief, I suffocated on question marks, symbols of the mind's attempt to
understand the chaos: *'Why me? Why this? Why now?'* I scoured
the past to look for origins, omens, offences, anything that
might count as a reason for the unreason that surrounded me,
something to act as a balm for the wound I had sustained,
something to link disparate events, a pattern I might superim-
pose on the random dots and dashes of my life.

2.   I was forced to abandon the techno-optimism of modern-
ity, I slipped through the net designed to counteract primitive
fears. I gave up reading daily papers or trusting the television, I
gave up faith in weather forecasts and economic indicators. My
thoughts made way for millenial disasters – earthquakes, floods,
devastation, plague. I came closer to the world of the gods, the
world of primitive forces guiding our lives. I felt the transience

of everything, the illusions upon which skyscrapers, bridges, theories, rocket launchers, elections and fast-food restaurants were built. I saw in happiness and repose a violent denial of reality. I looked commuters in the face and wondered why they had not seen. I imagined cosmic explosions, seas of lava flowing, pillage and destruction. I understood the pain of history, a record of carnage enveloped in nauseous nostalgia. I felt the arrogance of scientists and politicians, newscasters and petrol station attendants, the smugness of accountants and gardeners. I linked myself to the great outcasts, I became a follower of Caliban and Dionysus, and all who had been reviled for looking the pus-filled warts of truth in the face. In short, I briefly lost my mind.

3.   But did I have a choice? Chloe's departure had rocked the belief that I was master of my own house, it was a reminder of neuronal weakness, the conscious mind's impotence and inadequacy. I lost the pull of gravity, there was disintegration, and the curious lucidity that comes from total despair. I felt I had been unable to tell my own story, but had witnessed a demon do it for me, a childish, petulant demon who enjoyed raising his characters, then letting them crash down onto the rocks below. I felt like a puppet hooked on strings reaching up to the sky or deep into the psyche. I was a character in a master narrative whose grander design I was helpless to alter. I was the actor, not the playwright, blindly swallowing a script written in another's hand, ascribed an ending that hurtled me towards an unknown but painful end. I confessed and repented of the arrogance of previous optimisms, the belief the answer lay in thought. I realized the controls of the car had nothing to do

211

with its movements, I could press brakes and accelerators, but the vehicle continued with its own momentum. My temporary sense that the pedals had an effect was mistaken, my previous assurances had been nothing but a fortuitous coincidence between pedal and movement, conscious theories and fate.

4. If my own mind was a pale imitator and not initiator, then the real mind lay elsewhere, off-stage, below the set or up in the wings, not-mine mind. Once more I looked to destiny, once more I felt the divine nature of the origins of love. Both its arrival and departure [the first so beautiful, the second so gruesome] reminded me that I was but a plaything for the games of Cupid and Aphrodite. Unbearably punished, I sought out my guilt. I had been an unconscious criminal, treading on dangers I could not have suspected, killing without knowing it, a crime allowing no reprieve because it had been possessed of no conscious intention. I had meant love to live, I had killed it nevertheless. I had suffered a crime without knowing I had committed it, now I looked for the offence and, unsure of what I had done, confessed to everything. I tore myself apart looking for the weapon, every insolence returned to haunt me, acts of ordinary cruelty and thoughtlessness – none of these had been missed by the gods, who had now chosen to wreak their terrible revenge on me. I could not bear to look at my own face in the mirror, I tore my eyes out, waited for birds to peck at my liver and carried the weight of sins up mountains.

5. The ancient myths were dead of course, they were too large for the age of pocket calculators, Mount Olympus was a

ski resort, the Oracle of Delphi a taverna off Queensway – but the gods were still there, they had found new shape, put on suits and joined the modern age. They were now miniaturized, they fitted not into spaces between clouds, but into our psyche. I was living a drama in the stage of the mind, the individual the privileged seat of the gods' wrestlings. And at the centre, Zeus/ Freud, directing the show, ascribing motives, thunders, lightnings, curses. I was labouring under the curse of fate, not an external one, but a psycho-fate: a fate from within.

6.   In an age of science, psychoanalysis provided names for my demons. Though itself a science, it retained the dynamic [if not the substance] of superstition, the belief that the majority of life unfolds without adherence to rational control. In the stories of manias and unconscious motivations, compulsions and visitations, I recognized the world of Zeus and his colleagues, the Mediterranean transported to late-nineteenth-century Vienna, a secularized, sanitized view of much the same picture. Completing the revolution of Galileo and Darwin, Freud returned man to the initial humbleness of the Greek forefathers, the acted-upon rather than the actors. The Freudian world was made of double-sided coins one of whose sides we could never see, a world where hate could hide great love and great love hate, where a man might try to love a woman, but unconsciously be doing everything to drive her into another's arms. From within a scientific field that had for so long made the case for free will, Freud presented a return to a form of psychic determinism. It was an ironic twist to the history of science, Freudians questioned the dominance of the thinking 'I'

from within science itself. '*I think, therefore I am*,' had metamorphosed into Lacan's '*I am not where I think, and I think where I am not.*'

7.   There is no transcendental point from which we may observe the past, it is always constructed in the present, and changed along with its movements. Nor do we look at the past for its own sake, we do so rather in order to help us explain the present. The role my love for Chloe had played in my life came to seem very different now that things had finished so unhappily. In my optimistic moments within the relationship, I had slotted love into a narrative of an ever-improving life, proof that finally I was learning how to live and make myself happy. I recalled an aunt of mine, a part-time mystic, who had once predicted I would find contentment in love, most certainly with a girl who drew or painted. I remembered this aunt one day when watching Chloe sketching, charmed to see that even in this detail, Chloe was a fulfilment of the aunt's predictions. Walking arm in arm with her down the street, I sensed at times that the gods had blessed me, the happiness that had been conferred on me was evidence of a halo hovering above.

8.   If we look for omens, whether good or bad, we will never have trouble finding them. Now Chloe had left, a quite different love story raised its head, a love story doomed to fail, that had been chosen *because* it would fail, and that in its failure repeated a classic pattern of family neurosis. When my own parents had divorced, I recalled my mother warning me that I should be careful not to fall into a similar unhappy trap, because her mother had fallen into one, and her mother before that. Was

this not a hereditary disease, a curse placed on the family by our genetic and psychological make-up? A woman I had been seeing a couple of years before Chloe had once told me in the course of a bitter argument that I would never be happy in love because I 'thought too much'. It was true, I did think too much [these thoughts were proof enough]: the mind had shown itself to be as much an instrument of torture as a beneficial agent. Perhaps by thinking, I had unwittingly alienated Chloe with an arid analytical spirit so opposed to her own. I remembered reading a horoscope at the dentist, warning me that the harder I tried to succeed in love, the more difficult things could become. Rejection by Chloe came to seem part of a pattern whereby I would make efforts with a woman, only to watch things fall apart, on account of an as-yet obscure psychological fate. I could do nothing right, I had angered the gods, the curse of Aphrodite was upon me.

9.   The psycho-fatalism that replaced previous romantic fatalism were but two aspects of the same mind-set. They were both narrative modes, links in a chain of events that went beyond pure sequences of time, and valorized their direction along a good/bad scale, hero or tragic hero. Plotted on a graph [see Fig. 20.1], the first and happy narrative would have resembled an arrow moving up the scale, as I learnt to master the world and understand love.

10.   But Chloe's rejection had tainted this picture, reminding me that my past was complex enough to contain a very different account, one in which happiness would always be followed by a brutal downfall. Plotted on another graph [see Fig. 20.2], the

course of my life might appear as a range of peaks followed by ever deepening troughs – the life of a tragic hero, whose successes would always exact a most terrible price, culminating in life itself.

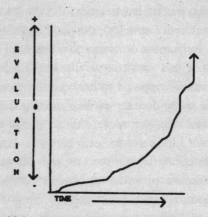

Figure 20.1   Hero Narrative [Romantic Fatalism]

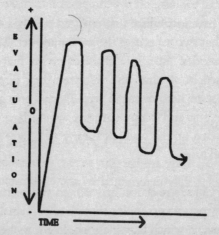

Figure 20.2   Tragic Hero Narrative [Psycho-fatalism]

216

11. The essence of a curse is that the person labouring under it cannot know of its existence. It is a secret code within the individual writing itself over a lifetime, but unable to find rational, preemptive articulation. Oedipus is warned by the Oracle that he will kill his father and marry his mother – but conscious warnings serve no purpose, they alert only the thinking 'I', they cannot defuse the coded curse. Oedipus is cast out from home in order to avoid the Oracle's prediction, but ends up marrying Jocasta nevertheless: his story is told for him, not by him. He knows the possible outcome, he knows the dangers, yet can change nothing: the curse defies the will.

12. But what curse did I labour under? Nothing other than an inability to form happy relationships, the greatest misfortune known in modern society. Exiled from the shaded grove of love, I would be compelled to wander the earth till the day of my death, unable to shake off my compulsion to make those I loved flee from me. I sought a name for this evil, and found it contained in the psychoanalytic description of *repetition compulsion*, defined as:

> . . . an ungovernable process originating in the uncon-
> scious. As a result of its actions, the subject deliberately
> places himself in distressing situations, thereby repeating
> an old experience, but he does not recall this prototype;
> on the contrary, he has the strong impression that the
> situation is fully determined by the circumstances of the
> moment.[8]

[8] *The Language of Psychoanalysis*, J. Laplanche, J. B. Pontalis, Karnac Books, 1988

13.   The comforting aspect of psychoanalysis [if one can talk so optimistically] is the *meaningful* world it suggests we live in. No philosophy is further from the thought that it is all a tale told by an idiot signifying nothing [even to deny meaning is meaningful]. Yet the meaning is never light: the psycho-fatalist's spell subtly replaced the words *and then* with the words *in order that*, thereby identifying a paralysing causal link. I did not simply love Chloe *and then* she left me. I loved Chloe *in order that* she leave me. The painful tale of loving her appeared as a palimpsest, beneath which another story had been written. Buried deep in the unconscious, a pattern had been forged, in the early months or years. The baby had driven away the mother, or the mother had left the baby, and now baby/man recreated the same scenario, different actors but the same plot, Chloe fitting into the clothes worn by another. Why had I even chosen her? It was not the shape of her smile or the liveliness of her mind. It was because the unconscious, the casting director of the inner drama, recognized in her a suitable character to fill the role in the mother/infant script, someone who would oblige the playwright by leaving the stage at just the right time with the requisite wreckage and pain.

14.   Unlike the curses of the Greek gods, psycho-fatalism at least held out the promise it could be escaped. Where id was, ego might be – if only ego had not been so crushed by pain, bruised, bleeding, punctured, unable to plan the day let alone the life. The ego had lost all powers of recuperation, it had been devastated by a hurricane, and struggled simply to restore basic services. Had I had the strength to rise from my bed, I might have made it to the couch, and there, Oedipus at Colonus,

begun to build an end to my sufferings. But I was unable to summon the necessary sanity to make it out of the house and seek help. I was unable even to talk or symbolize, I could not share my suffering with others, hence it ravaged me. I lay curled on the bed, the blinds drawn, irritated by the slightest noise or light, unduly upset if the milk in the fridge was stale or a drawer failed to open first time. Watching everything slip out of my grasp, I concluded the only way to regain at least a measure of control was to kill myself.

CHAPTER TWENTY-ONE

SUICIDE

1.   The Christmas season arrived, bringing with it carol singers, cards of good will and the first snowfalls. Chloe and I had been due to spend the Christmas weekend at a small hotel in Yorkshire. The brochure sat on my desk: 'Abbey Cottage welcomes its guests to warm Yorkshire hospitality in exquisite surroundings. Sit by the open fire in the oak-beamed living-room, take a walk along the moors, or simply relax and let us take care of you. A holiday at Abbey Cottage is everything you always wanted from a hotel – and more.'

2.   Two days before Christmas and hours before my death, at five o'clock on a sombre Friday evening, I received a call from Will Knott:

'I thought I'd ring to say goodbye, I'm due to fly back to San Francisco on the weekend.'

'I see.'

'Tell me, how are things with you?'

'I'm sorry?'

'Is everything all right?'

'All right? Well, yes, you could put it that way.'

'I was sorry to hear about you and Chloe. It's really too bad.'

'I was happy to hear about you and Chloe.'

'You've heard. Yeah, it just worked out. You know how much I always liked her, and she gave me a call and told me you guys had split up, and things moved from there.'

'Well, it's fantastic, Will.'

'I'm glad to hear you say it. I don't want this to get between us or anything, because a great friendship is not something I like to throw away. I always hoped you two could patch things up, I think you would have been great together, it's a real pity, but anyway. What are you doing over Christmas?'

'Staying home, I think.'

'Looks like you're going to get a real snowfall here, time to bring out the skis, eh?'

'Is Chloe with you now?'

'Is she with me now? Yes, no, I mean, she isn't actually with me right now. She was here, but she's just gone off to the store actually, we were talking about Christmas crackers, and she said she loved them, so she's gone to buy some.'

'That's great, give her my regards.'

'I'm sure she'd be delighted to hear we spoke. You know she's coming with me to spend Christmas in California?'

'Is she?'

'Yeah, it'll be great for her to see it. We'll spend a couple of days with my parents in Santa Barbara, then maybe go for a few days to the desert or something.'

'She loves deserts.'

'That's right, that's what she told me. Well, listen, I'd better leave you to it, and wish you a happy holiday. I've got to start sorting my stuff out around here. I may be back in Europe next fall, but anyway, I'll give you a call, and see how you're doing . . .'

3. I went into the bathroom and took out every last tablet I had collected, and laid them out on the kitchen table. With a mixture of aspirins, vitamins, sleeping pills, several glasses of cough syrup and whisky, I would have enough to end the whole charade. What more sensible reaction than this, to kill oneself after rejection in love? If Chloe really was my whole life, was it not normal that I should end that life to prove it was impossible without her? Was it not dishonest to be continuing to wake up every morning if the person I claimed was the meaning of existence was now buying Christmas crackers for a Californian architect with a house in the foothills of Santa Barbara?

4. My separation from Chloe had been accompanied by a thousand platitudinous sympathies from friends and acquaintances: it might have been nice, people drift apart, passion can't last for ever, better to have lived and loved, time will heal everything. Even Will managed to make it sound unexceptional, like an earthquake or a snowfall, something that nature sends to try us, and whose inevitability one should not think of challenging. My death would be a violent denial of normality – it would be a reminder that I would not forget as others had forgotten. I wished to escape the erosion and softening of time, I wished the pain to last for ever only so as to be connected to Chloe via its burnt nerve endings. Only by my death could I assert the importance and immortality of my love, only through self-destruction could I remind a world grown weary of tragedy that love was a deadly serious matter.

5.   The one reading this will be alive, but the author will be dead. It was seven o'clock, and the snow was still falling, starting to form a blanket over the city, the shroud. *It was the only way I could say I love you, I'm mature enough not to want you to blame yourself for this, you know how I feel about guilt. I hope you will enjoy California, I understand the mountains are very beautiful, I know you could not love me, please understand I could not live without your love* . . . The suicide text [writing as delayed suicide] had gone through many drafts: a pile of scrapped note-paper lay beside me. I sat at the kitchen table, wrapped in a grey coat, with only the shivering of the fridge for company. Abruptly, I reached for a tub of pills and swallowed what I only later realized had been twenty effervescent vitamin C tablets.

6.   I imagined Chloe receiving a visit from a policeman shortly after my inert body had been found. One could imagine the look of shock on her face, Will Knott emerging from the bedroom with a soiled sheet draped around him, asking, *'Is there anything wrong, darling?'* and she answering *'Yes, oh, God, yes!'* before collapsing into tears. The most terrible regret and remorse would follow – she would blame herself for not understanding me, for being so cruel, for being so shortsighted. Had any other man been so devoted to her as to take his own life for her?

7.   A notorious inability to express emotions makes human beings the only animals capable of suicide. An angry dog does not commit suicide, it bites the person or thing that made it angry, but an angry human sulks in its room and later shoots itself leaving a silent note. Man is the symbolic, metaphorical

creature: unable to communicate my anger, I would symbolize it in my own death. I would do injury to myself rather than injure Chloe, enacting by killing myself what I was suggesting she had done to me.

8.   My mouth was frothing now, orange bubbles breeding in its cavity and exploding as they came into contact with the air, spraying a light orange film over the table and the collar of my shirt. As I silently observed this acidic chemical spectacle, I was struck by the incoherence of suicide, namely that I did not wish to *choose* between being alive or dead. I simply wished to show Chloe that I could not, metaphorically speaking, live without her. The irony was that death would be too literal an act to grant me the chance to see the metaphor read, I would be deprived by the inability of the dead [in a secular framework at least] to look at the living looking at the dead. What was the point of making such a scene if I could not be there to witness others witnessing it? In picturing my death, I imagined myself in the role of audience to my own extinction, something that could never really happen in reality, when I would simply be dead, and hence denied my ultimate wish – namely, *to be both dead and alive*. Dead so as to be able to show the world in general, and Chloe in particular, how angry I was, and alive, so as to be able to see the effect that I had had on Chloe and hence be released from my anger. It was not a question of being or not being. My answer to Hamlet was to be *and* not to be.

9.   Those who commit a certain kind of suicide perhaps forget the second part of the equation, they look at death as an extension of life [a kind of after-life in which to watch the effect

of their actions]. I staggered to the sink and my stomach contracted out the effervescent poison. The pleasure of suicide was to be located not in the gruesome task of killing the organism, but in the reactions of others to my death [Chloe weeping at the grave, Will averting his eyes, both of them scattering earth on my walnut coffin]. To have killed myself would have been to forget that I would be too dead to derive any pleasure from the melodrama of my own extinction.

CHAPTER TWENTY-TWO

THE JESUS COMPLEX

1.   If there is any benefit to be found in the midst of agony, it may perhaps lie in the ability of certain sufferers to take this misery as evidence [however perverse] that they are special. Why else would they have been chosen to undergo such titanic torment other than to serve as proof that they are different, *and hence presumably better*, than those who do not suffer?

2.   I could not stand to be alone in my flat over the Christmas period, so I checked into a room in a small hotel off the Bayswater Road. I took with me a small suitcase and a set of books and clothes, but I neither read nor dressed. I spent whole days in a white bathrobe, lying on top of the bed and flicking through the channels of the television, reading room service menus and listening to stray sounds coming up from the street.

3.   There was at first very little to distinguish that noise from the general moan of the traffic below: car doors were screaming shut, lorries were grinding into first gear, a pneumatic drill was pounding the pavement. And yet above all that, I had begun to identify a quite different sound, rippling through the thin hotel wall from somewhere near my head, at that time pressed against a copy of *Time* magazine crushed against a sebaceous head-

board. It was becoming undeniable, however much one tried to deny it [and Heaven knows one might], that the sound from the next door room was none other than that of the mating ritual of the human species. 'Fuck,' I thought, 'they're fucking!'

4.   When a man hears others in the midst of such activity, there are certain attitudes one may reasonably expect him to adopt. If he is young and imaginative, he may willingly induce a process of identification with the male through the wall, constructing, with his poet's mind, an ideal of the fortunate woman – Beatrice, Juliet, Charlotte, Tess – whose screams he flatters himself to have induced. Or, if affronted by this objective recording of libido, he may turn away, think of England and raise the volume of the television.

5.   But my reaction was remarkable only for its passivity – or, rather, I failed to push reaction any way beyond acknowledgement. Since Chloe had left, I had done little but acknowledge. I had become a man who, in every sense of the word, could not be surprised. Surprise is, we are told by psychologists, a reaction to the unexpected, but I had come to expect everything, and could hence be surprised by nothing.

6.   What was passing through my mind? Nothing but a certain song heard once on the radio in Chloe's car, with the sun setting over the edge of the motorway:

> I'm in love, sweet love,
> Hear me calling out your name, I feel no shame,
> I'm in love, sweet love,
> Don't you ever go away, it'll always be this way.

I had grown intoxicated with my own sadness, I had reached the stratosphere of suffering, the moment where pain is raised into value and slides over into the Jesus Complex. The sound of the copulating couple and the song from happier days coalesced in the giant tears that had begun to flow at the thought of the misfortunes of my existence. But for the first time, these were not angry, scalding tears, rather the bitter-sweet taste of waters grown tinged with the conviction that it was not I, but the people who had made me suffer, who were so blind. I was elated, at the pinnacle where suffering brings one over into the valley of joy, the joy of the martyr, the joy of the Jesus Complex. I imagined Chloe and Will travelling through California, I listened to requests of 'more' and 'harder' from next door and grew drunk on the liquor of grief.

7.   'How great can one be if one is understood by everyone?' I asked myself, contemplating the fate of the Son of God. Could I really continue to blame myself for Chloe's inability to understand me? Her rejection was more a sign of how myopic she was than of how deficient I might have been. No longer was I necessarily the vermin and she the angel. She had left me for a third-rate Californian Corbusier because she was simply too shallow to understand. I began to reinterpret her character, concentrating on sides I found least pleasant. She was in the end very selfish, her charms only a superficial veneer masking a far less attractive nature. If she seduced people into thinking she was adorable, it had more to do with her amusing conversation and kind smile than any genuine grounds for love. Others did not know her the way I did and it was clear [though I had not realized it then] that she was inherently self-centred, rather

caustic, at times inconsiderate, often thoughtless, on occasion ungracious, when she was tired impatient, when she wanted her own way dogmatic, and in her decision to reject me, both unreflective and tactless.

8.   Grown infinitely wise through suffering, I could of course forgive, pity and patronize her for her lack of judgement – and to do so gave me infinite relief. I could lie in a lilac and green hotel room and be filled with a sense of my own virtue and greatness. I pitied Chloe for everything she could not understand, the infinitely wise seer who watches the ways of men and women with a melancholic, knowing grin.

9.   Why was my complex, the perverse psychological trick that turned every defeat and humiliation into its opposite, to be named after Jesus? I might have identified my suffering with that of Young Werther or Madame Bovary or Swann, but none of these bruised lovers could compete with Jesus's untainted virtue and his unquestionable goodness beside the evil of those he tried to love. It was not just the weepy eyes and sallow face attributed to him by Renaissance artists that made him such an attractive figure, it was that Jesus was a man who was kind, completely just *and* betrayed. The pathos of the New Testament, as much as of my own love story, arose out of the sad tale of a virtuous but misrepresented man, who preached the love of everyone for their neighbour but saw the generosity of his message thrown back in his face.

10.   It is hard to imagine Christianity having achieved such success without a martyr at its head. If Jesus had simply led a

quiet life in Galilee making commodes and dining tables and at the end of his life published a slim volume entitled *My Philosophy of Life* before dying of a heart attack, he would not have acquired the status he did. The agonizing death on the Cross, the corruption and cruelty of the Roman authorities, the betrayal by his friends, all these were indispensable ingredients for proof [more psychological than historical] that the man had God on his side.

11.   Feelings of virtue breed spontaneously in the fertile soil of suffering. The more one suffers, the more virtuous one must be. The Jesus Complex was entangled in feelings of superiority, the superiority of the underdog who appeals to a greater virtue in the face of the irresistible tyranny and blindness of his or her oppressors. Ditched by the woman I loved, I exalted my suffering into a quality [lying collapsed on a bed at three in the afternoon, Jesus on the Cross], and hence protected myself from experiencing my grief as the outcome of what was at best a mundane romantic break-up. Chloe's departure may have killed me, but it had at least left me in glorious possession of the moral high ground, condemned to death, but a martyr to history.

12.   The Jesus Complex lay at opposite ends of the spectrum from Marxism. Born out of self-hatred, Marxism prevented me from becoming a member of any club that would have me. The Jesus Complex still left me outside the club gates but, because it was the result of ample self-love, declared that I was not accepted into the club only because I was so special. Most clubs, being rather crude affairs, naturally could not appreciate the

great, the wise and the sensitive, who were to be left at the gates or dropped by their girlfriends. My superiority was revealed primarily on the basis of my isolation and suffering: *I suffer, therefore I am special. I am not understood, but for precisely that reason, I must be worthy of greater understanding.*

13.   In so far as it avoids self-hatred, one must have sympathy for the alchemy of weakness into virtue – and the evolution of my pain towards a Jesus Complex certainly implied a degree of good health. It showed that in the delicate internal balance between self-hatred and self-love, self-love was now winning. My initial response to Chloe's rejection had been a self-hating one, where I had continued to love Chloe while hating myself for failing to make the relationship work. But my Jesus Complex had turned the equation on its head, now interpreting rejection as a sign that Chloe was worthy of contempt or at best pity [that paragon of Christian virtues]. The Jesus Complex was nothing more than a self-defence mechanism, I had not wanted Chloe to leave me, I had loved her more than I had ever loved a woman, but now that she had flown to California, my way of accepting the unbearable loss was to reinvent how valuable she had been in the first place. It was clearly a lie, but honesty is sometimes more than we have strength for when, abandoned and desperate, we spend Christmas alone in a hotel room listening to the sound of orgasmic beatitude from next door.

CHAPTER TWENTY THREE

ELLIPSIS

1.   There is an Arabic saying that the soul travels at the pace of a camel. While we are forced ahead by the relentless dynamic of the timetabled present, our soul, the seat of the heart, trails nostalgically behind, burdened by the weight of memory. If every love affair adds a certain weight to the camel's load, then we can expect the soul to slow according to the significance of love's burden. By the time it was finally able to shrug off the crushing weight of her memory, Chloe had nearly killed my camel.

2.   With her departure had gone all desire to keep up with the present. I lived nostalgically, that is, with constant reference to my life as it had been with her. My eyes were never really open, they looked backwards and inwards to memory. I would have wished to spend the rest of my days following the camel, meandering through the dunes of memory, stopping at charming oases to leaf through images of happier days. The present held nothing for me, the past had become the only inhabitable tense. What could the present be next to it but a mocking reminder of the one who was missing? What could the future hold beside yet more wretched absence?

3.   When I was able to drown myself in memory, I would sometimes lose sight of the present without Chloe, hallucinating that the break-up had never occurred and that we were still together, as though I could have called her up at any time and suggested a film at the Odeon or a walk through the park. I would choose to ignore that she had decided to settle with Will in a small town in southern California, the mind would slip from factual reporting into a fantasy of the idyllic days of elation, love and laughter. Then, all of a sudden, something would throw me violently back into the Chloe-less present. The phone would ring and on my way to pick it up, I would notice [as if for the first time, and with all the pain of that initial realization] that the place in the bathroom where Chloe used to leave her hairbrush was now empty. And the absence of that hairbrush would be like a stab in the heart, an unbearable reminder that she had left.

4.   The difficulty of forgetting her was compounded by the survival of so much of the external world that we had shared together, and in which she was still entwined. Standing in my kitchen, the kettle might suddenly release the memory of Chloe filling it up, a tube of tomato paste on a supermarket shelf might by a form of bizarre association remind me of a similar shopping trip months before. Driving across the Hammersmith flyover late one evening, I would recall driving down the same road on an equally rainy night but with Chloe next to me in the car. The arrangement of pillows on my sofa evoked the way she placed her head down on them when she was tired, the dictionary on my book shelf was a reminder of her passion for

looking up words she did not know. At certain times of the week when we had traditionally done things together, there was an agonizing parallel between the past and present: Saturday mornings would bring back our gallery expeditions, Friday nights certain clubs, Monday evenings certain television programmes . . .

5.   The physical world refused to let me forget. Life is crueller than art, for the latter usually assures that physical surroundings reflect characters' mental states. If someone in a Lorca play remarks on how the sky has turned low, dark and grey, this is no longer an innocent meteorological observation, but a symbol of psychological states. Life gives us no such handy markers – a storm comes, and far from this being a harbinger of death and collapse, during its course, a person discovers love and truth, beauty and happiness, the rain lashing at the windows all the while. Similarly, in the course of a beautiful warm summer day, a car momentarily loses control on a winding road and crashes into a tree fatally injuring its passengers.

6.   But the external world did not follow my inner moods, the buildings that had provided the backdrop to my love story and that I had animated with feelings derived from it, now stubbornly refused to change their appearance so as to reflect my inner state. The same trees lined the approach to Buckingham Palace, the same stuccoed houses fronted the residential streets, the same Serpentine flowed through Hyde Park, the same sky was lined with the same porcelain blue, the same cars drove through the same streets, the same shops sold much the same goods to much the same people.

7.   Such a refusal of change was a reminder that the world did not reflect my soul, but was an independent entity that would spin on regardless of whether I was in love or out of it, happy or unhappy, alive or dead. The world could not be expected to change its expressions according to my moods, nor the great blocks of stones that formed the streets of the city to give a damn about my love story. Though they had been happy to accommodate my happiness, they had better things to do than to come crashing down now that Chloe was gone.

8.   Then, inevitably, I began to forget. A few months after breaking up with her, I found myself in the area of London in which she had lived and noticed that the thought of her had lost much of the agony it had once held, I even noticed that I was not primarily thinking of her [though this was exactly her neighbourhood], but of the appointment that I had made with someone in a restaurant near by. I realized that Chloe's memory had neutralized itself and become a part of history. Yet guilt accompanied this forgetting. It was no longer her absence that wounded me, but my growing indifference to it. Forgetting was a reminder of death, of loss, of infidelity to what I had at one time held so dear.

9.   There was a gradual reconquering of the self, new habits were created and a Chloe-less identity built up. My identity had for so long been forged around 'us' that to return to the 'I' involved an almost complete reinvention of myself. It took a long time for the hundreds of associations that Chloe and I had accumulated together to fade. I had to live with my sofa for months before the image of her lying on it in her dressing-

gown was replaced by another image, the image of a friend reading a book on it, or of my coat lying across it. I had to walk through Islington on numberless occasions before I could forget that Islington was not simply Chloe's district, but a useful place to shop or have dinner. I had to revisit almost every physical location, rewrite over every topic of conversation, replay every song and every activity that she and I had shared in order to reconquer them for the present, in order to defuse their associations. But gradually I forgot.

10. Time abbreviated itself, like an accordion that is lived in extension but remembered only in contraction. My life with Chloe was like a block of ice that was gradually melting as I carried it through the present, it was like a current event that becomes a part of history, and in the process contracts into a few central details. The process was like a film camera taking a thousand frames a minute, but discarding most of them, selecting according to mysterious whims, landing on a certain frame because an emotional state had coalesced around it. Like a century that is reduced and symbolized by a certain pope or monarch or battle, my love affair refined itself to a few iconic elements [more random than those of historians but equally selective]; the look on Chloe's face as we kissed for the first time, the light hairs on her arm, an image of her standing waiting for me in the entrance to Liverpool Street Station, her white pullover, her laugh when I told her my joke about the Russian in a train through France, her way of running her hand through her hair . . .

11. The camel became lighter and lighter as it walked through

time, it kept shaking memories and photos off its back, scattering them over the desert floor and letting the wind bury them in the sand, and gradually the camel became so light that it could trot and even gallop in its own curious way – until one day, in a small oasis that called itself the present, the exhausted creature finally caught up with the rest of me.

CHAPTER TWENTY-FOUR

LOVE LESSONS

1.   We must assume that there are certain lessons to be drawn from love, or else we remain happy to repeat our errors indefinitely, like flies that drive themselves insane butting their heads against window panes, unable to understand that though the glass may look clear, it cannot be flown through. Are there not certain basic truths to be learnt, shreds of wisdom that could prevent some of the excessive enthusiasms, the pain and the bitter disappointments? Is it not a legitimate ambition to become wise about love, in the way that one may become wise about diet, death or money?

2.   We start trying to be wise when we realize that we are not born knowing how to live, but that life is a skill that has to be acquired, like learning to ride a bicycle or play the piano. But what does wisdom counsel us to do? It tells us to aim for tranquillity and inner peace, a life free from anxiety, fear, idolatry and harmful passions. Wisdom teaches us that our first impulses may not always be true, and that our appetites will lead us astray if we do not train reason to separate vain from genuine needs. It tells us to control our imagination or it will distort reality and turn mountains into molehills and frogs into princesses. It tells us to hold our fears in check, so that we can

238

be afraid of what will harm us, but not waste our energies fleeing shadows on the wall. It tells us we should not fear death, and that all we have to fear is fear itself.

3.   But what does wisdom say about love? Is it something that should be given up completely, like coffee or cigarettes, or is it allowed on occasions, like a glass of wine or bar of chocolate? Is love directly opposed to everything that wisdom stands for? Do sages lose their heads or only overgrown children?

4.   If certain wise thinkers have given a nod of approval to love, they have been careful to draw distinctions between its varieties, in much the way that doctors counsel against mayonnaise, but allow it when it is made with low-cholesterol ingredients. They distinguish the rash love of a Romeo and Juliet from Socrates' contemplative worship of the Good, they contrast the excesses of a Werther with the bloodless brotherly love suggested by Jesus.

5.   The difference could be grouped into categories of *mature* and *immature* love. Preferable in almost every way, the philosophy of mature love is marked by an active awareness of the good and bad within each person, it is full of temperance, it resists idealization, it is free of jealousy, masochism or obsession, it is a form of friendship with a sexual dimension, it is pleasant, peaceful and reciprocated [and perhaps explains why most people who have known desire would refuse its painlessness the title of *love*]. Immature love on the other hand [though it has little to do with age] is a story of chaotic lurching between

239

idealization and disappointment, an unstable state where feelings of ecstasy and beatitude combine with impressions of drowning and fatal nausea, where the sense that one has finally found *the answer* comes together with the feeling that one has never been so lost. The logical climax of immature [because absolute] love comes in death, symbolic or real: the climax of mature love comes in marriage, and the attempt to avoid death via routine [the Sunday papers, trouser presses, remote-controlled appliances]. For immature love accepts no compromise, and once we refuse compromise, we are on the road to death. To someone who has known the pinnacles of immature passion, to settle for marriage is an unsustainable price – one would rather end things by driving a car over a cliff.

6.   With the naïve common sense that complex problems may elicit, I would sometimes ask [as though the answer could fit on the back of an envelope], 'Why can't we just all love one another?' Surrounded on every side by the agonies of love, by the complaints of mothers, fathers, brothers, sisters, friends, soap opera stars and hairdressers, I would hold out the hope that simply because everyone was inflicting and suffering from much the same pain, a common answer could be found – a metaphysical solution to the world's romantic problems on the grandiose scale of the Communists' answer to the inequities of international capital.

7.   I was not alone in my utopian day dream, joined there by a group of people, let me call them *romantic positivists*, who believed that with enough thought and therapy, love could be made into a less painful, indeed almost healthy, experience. This

assortment of analysts, preachers, gurus, therapists and writers, while acknowledging that love was full of problems, supposed that genuine problems must have equally genuine solutions. Faced with the misery of most emotional lives, romantic positivists would try to identify causes – a self-esteem complex, a father complex, a mother complex, a complex complex – and suggest remedies [regression therapy, a reading of the *City of God*, gardening, meditation]. Hamlet's fate could have been avoided with the help of a good Jungian analyst, Othello could have gotten his aggression out on a therapeutic cushion, Romeo might have met someone more suitable through a dating agency, Oedipus could have shared his problems in family therapy.

8.   Whereas art had a morbid obsession with the problems that attended love, romantic positivists threw the focus on the very practical steps that could be taken to prevent the most common causes of anguish and heartache. Next to the pessimistic views of much of Western romantic literature, the romantic positivists appeared as brave champions of a more enlightened and confident approach in an area of human experience traditionally left to the melancholy imagination of degenerate artists and psychotic poets.

9.   Shortly after Chloe left, I came across a classic of romantic positivist literature on a stand in a station bookshop, a work by a certain Dr Peggy Nearly that went by the title of *The Bleeding Heart*.[9] Though in a hurry to get back to my office, I bought the book nevertheless, attracted by a notice on its pink back

[9] *The Bleeding Heart*, Peggy Nearly, Capulet Books, 1987

cover that asked, 'Must being in love always mean being in pain?' Who was this Dr Peggy Nearly, a woman who could boldly claim to answer such a riddle? From the first page of the book, I learnt that she was

> ... a graduate of the Oregon Institute of Love and Human Relations, currently living in the San Francisco area, where she practises psychoanalysis, child therapy and marriage counselling. She is the author of numerous works on emotional addiction, as well as penis envy, group dynamics and agoraphobia.

10. And what was *The Bleeding Heart* about? It told the unfortunate yet optimistic story of men and women who fell in love with unsuitable partners, those who would treat them cruelly or leave them emotionally unfulfilled, or take to drink or become violent. These people had made an unconscious connection between love and suffering, and could not stop hoping that the unsuitable types they had chosen to adore would change and love them properly. Their lives would be ruined by the delusion that they could reform people who were by nature incapable of answering their emotional needs. By the third chapter, Dr Nearly had identified the roots of the problem as lying in deficient parents, who had given these unfortunate romantics a warped understanding of the affective process. If they had never loved people who were nice to them, it was because their earliest emotional attachments had taught them that love should be unreciprocated and cruel. But by entering therapy and being able to work through their childhood, they

might understand the roots of their masochism, and learn that their desire to change unsuitable partners was only the relic of a more infantile fantasy to convert their parents into proper care-givers.

11. Perhaps because I had finished reading it only a few days before, I found myself drawing an unlikely parallel between the plight of those described by Dr Nearly and the heroine of Flaubert's great novel, the tragic Emma Bovary. Who was Emma Bovary? She was a young woman living in the French provinces, married to an adoring husband whom she loathed because she had come to associate love with suffering. Conse-quently, she began to have adulterous affairs with unsuitable men, cowards who treated her cruelly and could not be depended upon to fulfil her romantic longings. Emma Bovary was ill because she could not stop hoping that these men would change and love her properly – when it was obvious that Rodolphe and Léon considered her as nothing more than an amusing distraction. Unfortunately, Emma lacked the oppor-tunity to enter therapy and become self-conscious enough to realize the origins of her masochistic behaviour. She neglected her husband and child, squandered the family money and in the end killed herself with arsenic, leaving behind a young child and a distraught husband.

12. It is sometimes interesting to think how differently events might have unfolded had certain contemporary solutions been available. What if Madame Bovary had been able to discuss her problem with Dr Nearly? What if romantic positivism had had

a chance to intervene in one of literature's most tragic love stories? One wonders at how the conversation would have flowed had Emma walked into Dr Nearly's San Francisco clinic.

[*Bovary on the couch, sobbing.*]

NEARLY: Emma, if you want me to help you, you'll have to explain what's wrong.

[*Without looking up, Madame Bovary blows her nose into an embroidered handkerchief.*]

NEARLY: Crying is a positive experience, but I don't think we should be spending the entire fifty minutes on it.

BOVARY: [speaking through her tears] He didn't write, he didn't . . . write.

NEARLY: Who didn't write, Emma?

BOVARY: Rodolphe. He didn't write, he didn't write. He doesn't love me. I am a ruined woman. I am a ruined pathetic, miserable, childish woman.

NEARLY: Emma, don't speak this way. I've told you already, you must learn to love yourself.

BOVARY: Why compromise by loving someone that stupid?

NEARLY: Because you are a beautiful person. And it's because you don't see it that you are addicted to men who inflict emotional pain.

BOVARY: But it was so good at the time.

NEARLY: What was?

BOVARY: Being there, with him beside me, making love to him, feeling his skin next to mine, riding through the woods. I felt so real, so alive, and now my life is in ruins.

NEARLY: Maybe you felt alive, but only because you knew it couldn't last, that this man didn't really love you. You hate your husband because he listens to everything you say, but you can't stop falling in love with the sort of man who will take two weeks to answer a letter. Quite frankly, Emma, your view of love betrays evidence of compulsion and masochism.

BOVARY: Does it? What do I know? I don't care if it's all a sickness, all I want is to kiss him again, to feel him holding me in his arms, to smell the perfume of his skin.

NEARLY: You have to start to make an effort to look inside yourself, to go over your childhood, then perhaps you will learn that you don't deserve all this pain. It's only because you grew up in a dysfunctional family in which your emotional needs were not met that you are stuck in this pattern.

BOVARY: My father was a simple farmer.

NEARLY: Perhaps, but he was also emotionally unreliable, so that you now respond to an unmet need by falling in love with a man who can't give you what you really want.

BOVARY: It's Charles that's the problem, not Rodolphe.

NEARLY: Well, my dear, we'll have to go on with this next week. It's coming to the end of your session.

BOVARY: Oh, Dr Nearly, I meant to explain earlier, but I won't be able to pay you this week.

NEARLY: This is the third time you tell me this sort of thing.

BOVARY: I apologize, but money is such a problem at the moment, I am so unhappy, I find myself spending it all on shopping. Just today, I went and bought three new dresses, a painted thimble and a china tea set.

13. It is hard to imagine a happy end to Madame Bovary's therapy, or indeed a much happier end to her life. It takes a fervent romantic positivist to believe that Dr Nearly [if she was ever paid] could have converted Emma into the well-adjusted, uncompulsive and caring wife that would have turned Flaubert's book into an optimistic tale of redemption through self-knowledge. Certainly Dr Nearly had an *interpretation* of Madame Bovary's problem, but there is a great difference between identifying a problem and solving it, between wisdom and the wise life. We are all more intelligent than we are capable, and awareness of the insanity of love has never saved anyone from

the disease. Perhaps the concept of wise or wholly painless love is as much of a contradiction as that of a bloodless battle – Geneva Conventions aside, it simply cannot exist. The confrontation between Madame Bovary and Peggy Nearly is the confrontation between romantic tragedy and romantic positivism. It is the confrontation between wisdom and wisdom's opposite, which is not the ignorance of wisdom [that is easy to put right], but the inability to act on the knowledge of what one knows is right. Knowing the unreality of our affair had proved to be of no help to Chloe and me, knowing we might be fools had not turned us into sages.

14. Rendered pessimistic by the intractable pains of love, I decided to turn away from it altogether. If romantic positivism could be of no help, then the only valid wisdom was the stoic advice never to fall in love again. I would henceforth retreat into a symbolic monastery, see no one, live frugally and throw myself into austere study. I read with admiration stories of men and women who had escaped earthly distractions, made vows of chastity, and spent their lives in monasteries and nunneries. There were stories of hermits who had endured life in caves in the desert for forty or fifty years, living only off roots and berries, never talking or seeing other human beings.

15. But sitting at a dinner party one evening, lost in Rachel's eyes while she outlined the course of her office life for me, I was shocked to realize how easily I might abandon stoic philosophy in order to repeat all the mistakes I had lived through with Chloe. If I continued to look at Rachel's hair tied elegantly in a

bun, or at the grace with which she used her knife and fork, or the richness of her blue eyes, I knew I would not survive the evening intact.

16.   The sight of Rachel alerted me to the limits of the stoic approach. Though love might never be painless and was certainly not wise, neither could it be forgotten. It was as inevitable as it was unreasonable – and its unreason was unfortunately no argument against it. Was it not absurd to retreat into the Judean hills in order to eat roots and shoots? If I wanted to be courageous, were there not greater opportunities for heroism in love? Moreover, for all the sacrifices demanded by the stoic life, was there not something cowardly within it? At the heart of stoicism lay the desire *to disappoint oneself before someone else had the chance to do so*. Stoicism was a crude defence against the dangers of the affections of others, a danger that it would take more endurance than a life in the desert to be able to face. In calling for a monastic existence free of emotional turmoil, stoicism was simply trying to deny the legitimacy of certain potentially painful yet fundamental human needs. However brave, the stoic was in the end a coward at the point of perhaps the highest reality, at the moment of love.

17.   We can always blind ourselves to the complexities of a problem by suggesting solutions that reduce the issue to a lowest common denominator. Both romantic positivism and stoicism were inadequate answers to the problems raised by the agonies of love, because both of them collapsed the question rather than juggle with its contradictions. The stoics had collapsed the pain and irrationality of love into a conclusive

argument against it – thereby failing to balance the undoubted trauma of our desires with the intractability of emotional needs. On the other hand, the romantic positivists were guilty of collapsing a certain easy grasp of psychological wisdom into a belief that love could be rendered painless for all, if only we learnt to love ourselves a little more – thereby failing to juggle a need for wisdom with the inherent difficulties of acting on its precepts, reducing the tragedy of Madame Bovary to an illustration of Dr Nearly's truistic theories.

18.   I realized that a more complex lesson needed to be drawn, one that could play with the incompatibilities of love, juggling the need for wisdom with its likely impotence, juggling the idiocy of infatuation with its inevitability. Love had to be appreciated without flight into dogmatic optimism or pessimism, without constructing a philosophy of one's fears, or a morality of one's disappointments. Love taught the analytic mind a certain humility, the lesson that however hard it struggled to reach immobile certainties [numbering its conclusions and embedding them in neat series] analysis could never be anything but flawed – and therefore never stray far from the ironic.

19.   Such lessons appeared all the more relevant when Rachel accepted my invitation for dinner the following week, and the very thought of her began sending tremors through the region the poets have called the heart, tremors that I knew could have meant one thing only – that I had once more begun to fall.